THE CHANCE OF LOVE

Book of Love, Book Seven

Meara Platt

ARE YOU SIGNED UP FOR DRAGONBLADE'S BLOG?

You'll get the latest news and information on exclusive giveaways, exclusive excerpts, coming releases, sales, free books, cover reveals and more.

Check out our complete list of authors, too!

No spam, no junk. That's a promise!

Sign Up Here

www.dragonbladepublishing.com

Dearest Reader;

Thank you for your support of a small press. At Dragonblade Publishing, we strive to bring you the highest quality Historical Romance from the some of the best authors in the business. Without your support, there is no 'us', so we sincerely hope you adore these stories and find some new favorite authors along the way.

Happy Reading!

CEO, Dragonblade Publishing

Additional Dragonblade books by Author Meara Platt

The Book of Love Series
The Look of Love
The Touch of Love
The Taste of Love
The Song of Love
The Scent of Love
The Kiss of Love
The Chance of Love

Dark Gardens Series
Garden of Shadows
Garden of Light
Garden of Dragons
Garden of Destiny

The Farthingale Series
If You Wished For Me (A Novella)

Also from Meara Platt
Aislin

CHAPTER ONE

London, England
October 1820

"HAD I KNOWN I was to have company, I would have dressed for the occasion," Captain Joshua Brayden said as he stepped naked out of his bath only to find Holly Farthingale staring at him wide-eyed, and her lovely mouth dropped open in shock.

"What?" She blinked like mad, her eyes resembling two blue flames flickering on a gusting breeze, as she tried to expunge the sight of him unclad.

They were standing in the kitchen of his cousin Romulus's home on Chipping Way, a home that was supposed to be unoccupied save for him. Or so he thought, or else he would not have started a fire in the kitchen hearth at midnight, boiled water for his bath, and rolled the tub before the fire to soak in it after his long journey.

Although the steaming water had helped relieve the tight coil of his muscles, his body still ached from days of hard riding. As he watched Holly by the golden glow of firelight, he worried his body would begin to ache for completely different reasons. "Turn around, Holly."

"Holy crumpets," she muttered, still staring at him. "What are you doing here?"

He glanced at the drying cloths stacked across the kitchen on one of the tables, then turned back to meet her gaze. "Trying to maintain my dignity. If you're not going to turn around, then close your eyes while I wrap that towel around me. Not that I particularly mind your staring. The towel is for your sake, not mine."

She gasped.

But still hadn't turned away.

Still hadn't shut her eyes, which were not the typical vibrant Farthingale blue. No, her eyes were an incredible swirl of blues, greens, and sadness.

"No one's supposed to be here," she said, sounding quite breathless.

He arched an eyebrow. "Then why are you?"

Since it appeared she wasn't going to close her eyes or turn around any time soon, he strode to the table and wrapped the cloth around the lower half of his body before approaching her.

She glanced at the door that was still ajar, allowing cold wind to blow in. He blocked her path and shut the door. Not that she seemed to want to flee, quite the opposite, she was rooted to her spot. "What is that you're clutching in your hands?" he asked.

It looked like a book with a faded, red-leather binding.

"Nothing." She tried to hide it behind her back, but the book was too big for her small hand. It slipped out of her grasp and fell to the floor.

He bent to pick it up and read its spine. *"The Book of Love."*

She groaned. "I came in here to hide it. Please give it back to me, Joshua...er, Captain Brayden."

"No need for formality, I should think." He wanted to laugh, but Holly was ashen except for her cheeks, which were a fiery pink. Odd, really. She was a young widow. Surely, she'd seen a naked man before.

But the girl looked as though she was coming undone.

The way she stared at him one would think she'd never been with a man before. "Why do you wish to hide it?"

She tore her gaze from his and looked down at her toes. "My family thinks it is time for me to consider marrying again." She shook her head furiously. "But I don't want to."

"Because you're not over the pain of his loss?" He couldn't even remember the man's name. She'd mentioned it once or twice.

Not that he cared to recall the name of the man who still held Holly's heart.

Sorrow radiated off this girl...woman...young and fragile beauty. He considered reaching out to take her in his arms but resisted the urge. His body was still wet since he hadn't bothered to dry himself off before wrapping the towel around his waist. Droplets trailed down his neck, chest, and arms, but he ignored them. "You've been a widow several years now. Perhaps they're right. It will be a long and lonely life for you if you insist on clinging to the past instead of looking forward."

He knew she'd have no trouble finding a new husband for herself. The girl was beautiful in a sad and haunting way. Well, she could also be vibrant and captivating when she wanted to be. He'd seen her in those few instances when she was laughing and chattering with her cousins.

He brushed a stray curl off her brow. "Perhaps you ought to consider reading the book instead of trying desperately to hide it."

She tipped her chin up in indignation, but the gesture only brought attention to her big eyes and exceptionally pretty mouth. "What makes you think I'm desperate?"

"Other than the fact you stole in here after midnight, wearing only your nightgown and robe. You have bedroom slippers on your feet. Obviously, you waited for everyone in your family to fall asleep before stealing in here like a thief in the night."

"Violet is my cousin. Now that she is married to your cousin, Romulus, this house is as much hers as it is his."

"Ah, quite so. But it is not your house. You are breaking in."

"Only to bury this book where it will never be found again." She cleared her throat. "Well, perhaps you're right. But I only meant to keep it hidden until they gave up on me and were ready to ask for it back. This book should have gone to one of my sisters. They're the ones in need of husbands."

"And you sincerely believe you're not?" Her golden curls were held back in a loose braid that fell below her nicely shaped bottom. What man would not wish to unbind that braid and bury his fingers in those long, silken strands?

What man wouldn't wish to bury himself inside her?

Not him, of course. He tamped down the errant thought.

Holly was the sort of girl one married.

He was in no hurry to have a ring put through his nose and led to the altar. Quite the opposite, he'd reached a comfortable plateau in his life. A rewarding position as a respected officer in the King's First Dragoon Guards working as the War Ministry's military liaison to Parliament. A decent income from his service and other Brayden family investments. All the women a man could possibly want or handle at one time.

Indeed, he did not lack for female companionship whenever he felt the need. "Holly, why are you so closed off to the possibility of love? Your cousins have faith in that book, since it seems to have worked its magic on them and their husbands. I can attest to that fact, having seen two Brayden men conquered. Romulus took about a minute and a half to fall in love with Violet. Finn took perhaps less than that to fall in love with your cousin, Belle."

"What are you suggesting? That you and I—"

"No." Lord help him, he hadn't meant for him and Holly to race to the altar. Not that she wasn't irresistible. Perhaps it was not wise for them to be standing alone, him with no clothes on, and she with an easily untied robe and thin nightrail.

It would take him to the count of five to have those bedclothes off her, perhaps less time if he kept his full attention on the task. "I'm just pointing out this book seems to have worked its magic on them. Not just them, also on your cousin, Poppy, and her friends."

She nodded. "All of England was abuzz when Olivia Gosling brought the mighty Beast to heel. Penelope Sherbourne wound up with the Scot of her dreams, Thad MacLauren."

"Robbie MacLauren works with me in the halls of Parliament."

She rolled her eyes. "He has an awful reputation with the ladies."

Joshua chuckled. "He has an excellent reputation among some ladies, but they're not the sort one would ever introduce to one's family. The point is, this book seems to have helped make happy marriages for your cousins and their friends. You ought to be embracing it, not be afraid of it."

"No." She shook her head. "No, I cannot."

Sighing, he held it out to her. "Take it, Holly. But I really think you ought to read it."

"I have a better idea. You keep it." She put her hand over his to stop him from returning it to her. "Perhaps it works for men, too."

She removed her hand as though his touch suddenly burned. "I know you're not keen to take a bride yet. But you will be eventually. Why not prepare yourself now? Read it. Whenever you are ready to marry, you'll have a good idea of the sort of girl you want as your wife. Perhaps you'll find a duke's daughter for yourself."

He laughed. "No, someone like that is too far above my station."

"But isn't this the entire point of the book? You've just said so yourself. Poppy's friend Olivia got her Duke of Hartford. Poppy got her Earl of Welles. Honey got her Earl of Wycke. Why cannot Joshua Brayden aim as high as he wishes?"

His thoughts were not on settling down with one woman. But this book could be used to his advantage. Why not? He could enjoy a feast of women using its knowledge. Seduce whomever he pleased. There were plenty of debutantes from the highest ranks who were beautiful and willing. A surprising number of them were not virgins.

He seemed able to tell the innocents from those who were merely feigning innocence. So why not go for a higher class of bedmate? Especially if he kept to the ones already initiated to the pleasures of the body.

He stared at Holly.

Well, he wasn't always on the mark about innocence. She had been married. Her husband must have…at least once or twice during their marriage. Yet, she had the look of a girl untouched.

"Please, keep it for now." She placed her hand over his once more. "Just promise to place it somewhere safe and give it back to me when I ask for it."

He nodded. "You have my oath."

They were standing so close, he caught the scent of lavender on her delicate skin and the smell of mint tea on her lips.

"Thank you, Joshua." She reached up to kiss him lightly on the cheek, then opened the door and hurried out.

He'd been ambushed once or twice while fighting enemy forces and recalled the physical changes that came over him in the heat of such battles. The sudden surge of fire in his blood, the thunderous pounding of his heart, and heightening of his senses.

This is what he now felt after Holly's kiss. Fire. Thunder. Exhilaration.

How is it possible?

He was still struggling to bring his body under control when the door opened again to reveal a slightly out of breath Holly.

Had she just experienced the same torrid response and sought more? A quick tumble? "Joshua, I need you."

"I need you, too."

"What?"

Oh, Lord! She had no idea what he was talking about. "What?"

She eyed him dubiously. "I need your help in getting back over the wall."

She pointed to the tall, stone wall between Romulus's house and the Farthingale house. Romulus resided at Number One Chipping Way. The Farthingales resided at Number Three. They stood staring at each other, Joshua suddenly all too aware of her. "Do you mean to say you scaled the wall between the homes. Why didn't you just walk over?"

"The gates are locked. This was the simplest way to do it."

He folded his arms over his chest and grinned at her. "Not so simple if you're now stuck and can't climb back over."

"I can do it." She pursed her lips and frowned at him. "I just have to drag one of the kitchen stools to the wall. You see, there's a bench on the other side. I used it to help me over the wall and then merely dropped to this side. But I'll need the same help getting over from this side. Would you be so kind as to return the stool where it properly belongs once I'm through using it?"

"No. You don't need it. I'll lift you up."

Her cheeks were on fire again. "I don't think it is necessary or appropriate."

"Seriously? Appropriate? You've just seen me stark, raving naked."

She cleared her throat. "Yes, um...well, I do hope you'll take this little misunderstanding to the grave. Never mention it again. Not to anyone. Ever."

He didn't respond.

She sighed. "You're the one who'll be dragged to the altar and forced to marry me if word ever gets out. It's no skin off my nose. I'll have a nice-looking husband, and everyone will stop bothering me about this marriage business."

"I thought you didn't want to be married."

"I don't."

He cast her a lazy smile. "But you'd muddle through if you had to marry me. I gather you enjoyed the sight of my body."

"No! I...just get out of my way. If you're not going to carry the stool for me, I'll do it myself."

He caught her about the waist and led her outside. "I just told you, I'll lift you over."

What was it about this girl's body that had him in flames again? All he did was touch her innocently—one hand on her clothed waist.

The night was cold, but you couldn't tell it from him.

He was sweating. "Here, use my hands as a foothold."

"Oh, I see. And then you can lift me so I can easily reach the top."

Which was a workable plan until she raised her robe and nightgown to her knees and propped her foot, which happened to be attached to an exquisitely shaped leg, onto his hands. She clutched his shoulders, then his head. "Holly, grip the wall, not my head."

"I'm afraid to let go. Don't raise me so quickly." She gave a muffled cry as she lost her balance.

Her bosom fell into his face.

Her foot fell out of his handhold.

Her body slid down his, her soft, plump breasts blazing a trail of fire down his chest. As if that wasn't enough, she took down his towel at the same time her nightclothes slid upward so that he felt too much of her leg against his thighs, and he didn't want to think about what more dangerous parts of him she felt against her silky thighs.

Thank the Graces, the cold had chilled his arousal just enough to keep her from screaming like a banshee in alarm. "Holly, I..." He didn't know what to say, so he just laughed softly.

"Joshua, this isn't funny! You're naked again!" she said in an emphatic whisper.

"Whose fault is that?" He bent to retrieve his towel and felt her staring at his arse. "Holly, close your eyes."

"What?" She gasped and planted her hands over her eyes. "You are a horrible man. How did we get in this ridiculous situation anyway? Never mind, don't answer that. Just keep that book safe, and get me over the wall without killing me in the process."

"Right, let's try this again." He secured the towel around himself and then made a foothold for her with his hands. "Put one hand on my shoulder, and as I slowly lift you, take hold of the top of my head to steady yourself." He raised her a little higher. "Now, grab hold of the wall with one hand."

"I'm afraid to let go of you."

"Bollocks, don't start this again. You can do it. I have you. I won't let you fall."

"All right, but don't move."

"I won't. Good. Now put the other hand on the wall. Excellent. Keep hold of the wall."

He slowly raised her a little higher, meaning to issue more instructions, but her body fell against his mouth at just that moment. He almost expired when he realized his lips were resting against the junction of her thighs.

Was she purposely trying to kill him?

Thank goodness there were two layers of fabric between her *pearl* and his lips.

His jaw began to twitch.

Was it possible she was doing this on purpose? Teasing him? Arousing him?

Then she accidentally kicked him in the face as she swung her legs over.

Did Hannibal have such logistical problems when crossing the Alps with his elephants? "Holly, are you all right? Did you make it over safely?"

She cried out softly and then grunted. "Yes, fine. Just slipped off the bench. Landed on my backside."

"Are you hurt. I'll come over and—"

"Don't you dare! Stay on your side of the wall. I'll climb back into my room now."

"Climb?" He leaped up onto the wall just as she struggled to her feet. Waving to him to hold him back, she tiptoed over to an oak tree whose branches were spread wide and extended quite close to the house. One could easily sneak in and out of that upper-floor bedchamber from those branches without being noticed.

He watched her lift her nightclothes to her thighs as she began to climb. His heart shot into his throat. Her legs were magnificent by moonlight. But he was worried because she did not have a lot of upper body strength. Lord help him, she was soft and slight. He didn't want her falling.

He remained watching her, wanting to scale the wall and help her up the tree, but it would not do to be caught with Holly in his arms. She wasn't used to stealing about in the night, but she made it safely in through the window in a headfirst tumble. He hoped she had not bruised her lovely body too severely.

He waited several moments longer to be sure she had not awakened the entire Farthingale household. All remained quiet, so he eased himself down from the wall and returned inside the house.

The book was sitting atop the table.

He growled at it. "You planned this, didn't you?"

The book sat silent.

He continued to stare at it.

"Bollocks," he said, running a hand through his wet hair. "I'm in trouble, aren't I?"

He could have sworn the book laughed at him.

CHAPTER TWO

HOLLY'S HEART POUNDED wildly as she removed her slippers and robe and crept back into bed. *Oh. My. Heavens.* She settled on her back and gazed up at the ceiling, hoping to see nothing but blackness. Unfortunately, Joshua's magnificently naked body had been etched into her still throbbing eyeballs, so this is what she saw looking back at her from the ceiling.

His sculptured splendor.

She turned her face to the wall, but he was there as well, his muscled torso wet and glistening in the amber glow of firelight.

She squeezed her eyes shut.

No. Still there.

But as humiliating as her midnight adventure had been, it had served an important purpose. She now knew what a man's body looked like.

All of it.

From the broad shoulders, muscled arms, and dusting of dark gold hair across his firm chest. Taut leanness of his waist and chiseled contours of his legs. But it was that part of him between his legs that she had been most curious about.

Now she knew what a man looked like *there.*

Knew it and could not stop thinking about it.

She had also *felt* him because she'd been so clumsy trying to scale the wall. But touching Joshua had proved to be her undoing, putting her hand to his warm, wet skin and feeling the ripple of his muscles as she clung to his shoulders while he tried to raise her.

Then she'd accidentally slid down the front of him.

Her body had come alive at that moment.

This is what a man felt like.

Hard and warm.

The scent of him was also intoxicating, for he'd just come out of his bath. She'd inhaled when he'd stepped close, taking in the scent of sandalwood soap and steaming water. But beneath those scents was Joshua's own clean and rugged essence.

She thought she'd expire when those glistening droplets of water began to trail down his chest. She wanted to lick them off him. Of course, he would have considered her a lunatic and pushed her away.

"Holly, is something wrong? You're tossing and turning quite furiously. Were you having a bad dream?"

"No, Violet. I'm fine. Just a little restless." Her cousin was sharing a guest bedchamber with her since Romulus was away, and Violet did not like to be alone next door in that big house. Also, she had expected to be in Plymouth with Romulus, but her plans had changed. They had arranged weeks ago for Joshua to stay at their house upon his return to London.

But now that their plans had changed and Joshua had no way of knowing, Violet had made herself comfortable here. "All right. Just wake me if you think you're falling ill. You don't sound quite your-self."

Crumpets.

"Good night, Violet. I'm feeling better now." As well as one could feel with a naked man still etched into one's eyeballs.

By morning, Holly was much calmer.

Or so she hoped.

She'd washed, then dressed in an ecru morning gown trimmed with copper-brown ribbon. She allowed her maid, a pretty girl by the name of Agnes, to style her hair in a twisted braid that gathered at the nape of her neck. She often wore her hair this way, for it was simple and yet, elegant.

Much of the family was already in the dining room, having their breakfast. The silver salvers were set out across the massive buffet, and the delightful aroma of warm bread, *oeufs a la coque*, kippers, and glazed ham tickled her nostrils and heightened her appetite.

Seated at each end of the table were her aunt and uncle, Sophie and John. Also seated at the table was their prune-faced, maiden aunt, Hortensia, who would be quite pretty for an older woman if she ever smiled. She had a cutting wit and a no-nonsense way about her, but despite being a bit of a curmudgeon, they all adored her.

Heather and Dahlia, the sisters Holly had been assigned to chaperone, had just finished ladling food onto their plates and took seats beside Violet, who was slathering apricot jam on her bread.

"Good morning," Holly said, taking up a plate and placing one kipper, one egg, and one slice of bread on it. When she sat, a footman came over to pour her a cup of tea.

Violet turned to her. "Are you feeling any better this morning?"

"What's wrong, Holly? Did you not sleep well? Are you ill?" Her sisters tossed the questions at her at the same time.

"Oh, dear," Sophie said. "John, perhaps you ought to send for George."

"This London chill cuts through one's bones," Hortensia intoned. "I do hope you aren't feverish. You do look a bit flush."

"I'm fine. No need to send for Uncle George." He was John's brother and one of London's most brilliant doctors. Perhaps the most brilliant doctor in all of England. "Not feverish either."

Until Joshua was announced by the family butler, Pruitt, and balls of fire shot into her cheeks. "Captain Joshua Brayden."

He strode in like a golden-haired warrior, utterly magnificent in his neatly pressed uniform and highly polished Hessians. He had shining medals pinned to his broad chest.

Even dressed, he took one's breath away.

He also wore a smile that could melt a glacier. "Good morning. Mr. Farthingale, I hope you don't mind the intrusion, but I arrived late last night and wished to let Violet know I am here." He turned to Holly's cousin. "I did not realize your plans had changed, but I wanted to assure you that I will move out immediately."

"Oh, no. Please stay." Violet cast him a cheerful smile. "You are more than welcome to the run of the house. I shall pop in and out throughout the day to gather one thing or another, but you are to treat the house as yours. I've moved back in with Uncle John and Aunt Sophie for the next week because my cousins are here, and it is so much more fun to be with them than alone in that big, rattling house. Besides, I shall be off to Plymouth within the week. No point upsetting the plans."

"Well, let me know if you have a change of heart. It's your home, and I wish to respect that."

"Thank you, but I'm perfect right here. Holly and I are sharing a room. Heather and Dahlia are right next door."

"Have a seat, Joshua," John said. "Join us for breakfast."

His chuckle was rich and hearty. "I'd like that."

Of course, a man his size needed to be fed.

Holly watched as he went to the buffet and filled his plate.

When he turned and pinned her with a steady gaze, she realized the chair next to hers was unoccupied, and he meant to take it. *No, no, no!* There were several other empty seats around the table.

Don't sit next to me.

Don't sit here.

Don't.

"How are you, Holly?" he asked, drawing out the chair next to hers and settling his large frame into it. He grazed her shoulder as he did so. Had he done it on purpose? Or was he simply a big man and took up more space?

"Coffee, please," he said to the footman attending him but immediately turned back to her. "Have you been enjoying London?"

Gad, these Braydens were the size of gladiators. Big and gloriously muscled. "Yes, very much."

Dahlia frowned at her. "She's hardly gone out."

"Not so! I go out all the time with you and Heather. We visit our other cousins, stop over at Lady Dayen's home almost every day, and make regular stops at the modiste. We've visited museums and attended teas, musicales, and other evening parties."

Dahlia rolled her eyes. "You sit with the old ladies at every affair, and where there's dancing, you never dance."

All eyes were on her, including those of the man beside her. She felt as though she were a criminal brought in for questioning. Why couldn't they leave her alone and let her shrink into the background? "I'm your chaperone, Dahlia. Not one of the debutantes."

Joshua regarded her thoughtfully. "We'll have to remedy that. Save me a waltz at Lord Milford's tonight. It's hardly a grand ball in the style of Lord Forster's, but it should be quite merry." He turned to her sisters. "Well, I've claimed a dance from Holly. Now I'll claim one from each of you."

Dahlia and Heather giggled like two peahens.

"Thank you, Captain Brayden," Heather said. "We'd be delighted."

"Holly, are you certain you're not feverish?" Hortensia intoned. "Your face looks like it is on fire."

"Perhaps she's overcome by Captain Brayden's nearness," Violet teased.

Holly choked on her tea, her fit of coughing rendering her unable to reply, which she would have done with priggish indignation. Perhaps it was better not to say anything. Her sisters and cousin would only subject her to more teasing.

Now Joshua's arm was around her shoulders, warm and comforting as he offered his handkerchief. "Here, Holly. Take this."

He appeared to be genuinely concerned.

The cad.

She knew deep down he had to be laughing at her.

But she took his handkerchief and blew into it, hoping to calm herself.

"Better?" he asked as her coughs died down.

She nodded, although she wasn't really. This new awareness had come upon her so suddenly and with stunning force. She didn't know what to make of it or of Joshua. They'd met only a short while ago in Oxford when he'd gone there with his brother to help her Oxford cousins defend their perfume business against some very nasty villains.

She liked him, of course.

And did feel quite badly about almost killing him...well, almost knocking him unconscious at their first meeting. Obviously, he'd recovered fully.

Thank goodness.

She wasn't one for violence. However, the roiling feeling in her stomach and fire coursing through her body could only be described as almost that, certainly reckless and tumultuous. Was this what her cousins meant when they spoke of passion?

"No, not quite better, are you?" Joshua said quietly against her ear.

"No," she whispered back, unable to say more.

She'd had no passion in her marriage to Walter Gleason, a young man from one of York's finest families. They'd known each other since childhood and always got along well. She was surprised when he'd offered marriage, for she was only seventeen at the time. He was pleasant company but had never shown her any particular preference.

Perhaps she and her parents were so taken with her good fortune, they didn't give his offer sufficient consideration. Her father had given his consent immediately. She was almost eighteen by the time their wedding ceremony was held.

In all those months leading up to the wedding, her mother had never talked to her about the wedding night or what a husband should expect from a wife. They'd chatted circles around it, and Holly did not find any of their conversation helpful.

As it turned out, the talk wasn't necessary.

Walter had not touched her that first night.

Nor had he touched her on any other night of their marriage.

"Please excuse me." She knocked over her chair in her haste to get away, almost tripping over it had Joshua not caught her. Wordlessly, he set the chair upright and drew it away to give her passage.

She ran out of the dining room.

Her first thought was to return to her bedchamber, but then she'd be trapped if Violet and her sisters came up after her. She ran outside instead, intending only to sit in the garden until she regained her composure.

But the day was cool, and she hadn't thought to bring a shawl.

No matter, she wouldn't remain out here very long, and the bite to the breeze was refreshing. She glanced down at her hands and realized she still held Joshua's handkerchief. Having used it to wipe her dripping nose, she could not simply hand it back to him. She used the sleeve of her gown to wipe her tears. Not that she was crying, but her eyes had watered while she was coughing.

She sat on the bench that stood against the wall, the one she'd used to climb over last night, and stared blankly at the garden. The trees were starting to lose their leaves, so many branches were bare. Those that were not held leaves of beautiful reds and golds.

The flower beds were sparse, only the hardier blooms surviving, the reds and golds she thought of as autumn colors. Had she made a mistake in giving that book on love away?

She'd only given it to Joshua, so it was in safe hands. He would return it to her whenever she asked. But she had to think about whether she wanted it back. Hadn't she managed quite well all these years by suppressing all feelings?

She'd made a fool of herself at the breakfast table when those feelings had suddenly burst forth. It was humiliating, but also a little bit exhilarating. Perhaps she'd think about venturing out from her protective walls once Dahlia and Heather had made fine matches for themselves. To do so now would risk ruining their marriage prospects, especially if her foolish behavior occurred in public.

"Holly, there you are." Joshua strode toward her and propped a foot on the bench rather than take the seat beside her. She was grateful for his maintaining a modest distance.

"Yes, indeed. Here I am." She waved her hand airily, hoping to sound cheerful. But Joshua had quite the discerning gaze. Little ever seemed to get past him.

He cast her a worried frown. "What's wrong?"

"Other than my ridiculous behavior this morning? And even more foolish behavior last night?"

He cast her an affectionate smile that melted her bones. "You were nothing of the sort. You were caught by surprise last night and are still feeling the aftereffects. Don't be so hard on yourself. Why do you think soldiers train rigorously? It is precisely because we have to learn to overcome these natural responses when ambushed or suddenly confronted with an unexpected situation."

She snorted. "Is this why you've shown nothing but calm and poise, while I've been flapping my wings like a demented hen?"

He chuckled. "You are hardly that. But yes, I've learned to overcome the instinct to freeze like a doe caught in a hunter's line of fire. I've also learned to keep my wits about me instead of allowing them to scatter."

"You were brilliant at Oxford," she said, referring to the swift and efficient manner he and his brother had brought down those villains. While his brother Finn had been brilliant in protecting her cousin Belle, Joshua had been the one to lead his regiment into battle against the criminal elements. Their evil tentacles had spread wide throughout Oxford, and it was no easy feat to lop all those moving arms of greed, extortion, and corruption off at once.

He shrugged off the compliment. "This is what the army pays me to do."

"Does it also pay you to dance with hopeless widows?"

"No, this I do for myself. If you don't attend Lord Milford's tonight, I will climb up to your bedchamber, drag you out of bed, and claim my waltz right there."

"You wouldn't dare!"

But she knew by the gleam in his eyes that he would do exactly that. Violet, who shared her room, would be opening the window for him and cheering him on.

She frowned at him. "That is beastly and cruel."

"No, Holly. I would never hurt you. But someone has and left you with deep scars. I don't recall the name of your husband. Sorry. But this misery you're feeling has to do with him. I thought it was because you loved him deeply."

She gripped the edge of bench, both hands clutching tightly so that her knuckles turned white. "What makes you think I didn't?"

CHAPTER THREE

*M*OTHER IN HEAVEN.

Joshua shook his head, trying to make sense of the thoughts now whirling madly between his ears. Was it possible Holly did not love the man she'd married? How did he not see this earlier? He'd assumed hers was a love match because this was the Farthingale way, to marry for love.

But she had been quite young at the time, perhaps mistaken in her feelings. How would someone like Holly react to the realization her marriage was not one built on love?

Damn it. She'd hide in shame. She'd put the blame on herself for failing her husband and punish herself for the rest of her life.

However, this did not quite explain the aura of innocence he'd sensed about her last night. As a married woman, she would have had a physical relationship with her husband. Perhaps an unhappy one, so that over time he'd stopped seeking her bed. Well, it was none of his business what they'd done in the marriage.

He crossed his arms over his chest. "What's it to be? Will you attend Lord Milford's party and dance with me?"

She frowned at him. "Do you leave me a choice?"

"No." He wasn't sorry for it either. "I'll see you this evening. Have a nice day, Holly."

Turmoil radiated off her slender body. He could see pain, hurt, anger, and even a little bit of excitement reflected in the haunted pools of her eyes.

It was time someone stirred a little excitement in that prim lass.

Lord, how could someone so buttoned-up shoot fire through his blood the way she did?

He left her seated in the garden, her small hands still clutching the bench in a death grip, and walked onto Chipping Way. Since the Houses of Parliament would be quiet for the next few weeks while the lords fled north to hunt grouse, he stopped back at Romulus's house to retrieve that book on love Holly had been so desperate to hide.

There wouldn't be much for him to do all day, so where was the harm in taking it to his office for a bit of reading?

Which is what he was doing when his brother Ronan and their friend Robert MacLauren stepped into his office later that afternoon and made themselves at home, despite the fact that he hadn't invited them to stay. "Get out."

"Do ye have anything decent to drink?" Robbie asked, walking to Joshua's files and beginning to rummage through them. "Och, nothing but papers in here. Where's yer bottle, Josh?"

"I don't have one." He shut the book and set it aside on his desk.

Ronan groaned. "Not a drop to ease a man's thirst? I think I'll go mad if I have to put up with another two weeks of this."

The three of them were men of action. Having nothing to do but roam the empty halls of Parliament made them restless. Ronan was a captain in the Royal Navy, working as the Admiralty's liaison to Parliament. Robbie was a captain in the Royal Scots Dragoons, working as the Scottish liaison to Parliament. Since Joshua was the army liaison, the three of them often worked together.

He and Ronan had always been close, other than the occasional brotherly spat that amounted to nothing. Robbie had become a good friend of theirs over the course of their assignments.

"I have a bottle of bootleg port in my office," Robbie said.

Ronan nodded. "Splendid. I'll fetch a few glasses from the conference room."

"Fine." Joshua glanced at the book he'd been forced to set aside. It was interesting, and he'd hardly gotten halfway through it. He had hoped to finish it before he danced with Holly, but that would not happen now.

Instead of immediately walking out, the two approached his desk. Ronan picked up the book before he could stop him. "What is this you're reading, Josh?"

"None of your business. Give it back." Which was the worst thing he could have said since it only piqued their curiosity. Ronan held it out of his reach when he tried to grab it from his hands.

"Blessed Scottish saints!" Robbie burst out laughing. *"The Book of Love?"*

"Josh, have you suffered brain damage?" Ronan had an irritating smirk on his face. "Love? As in leg-shackled, parson's noose, ring through the nose, ballbusting—"

"Your point is made, Ronan. Enough."

His brother opened it and flipped through the pages. "Is this the book that felled Finn and Romulus?"

Robbie's eyes widened in surprise. "Not to mention, my cousin Thad. Yes, it must be. I'd know that faded red binding anywhere. What in bloody blazes are you doing with it?"

"What does it matter? I've been entrusted with it, and I've decided to read it."

Robbie shook his head. "Why?"

"Why not?"

Ronan held up a hand. "Wait. Not another word about this book until we return with a bottle and glasses."

Joshua had no lock on his door, so he settled back in his chair and put his feet up atop his desk, ready to endure an afternoon of taunts from these two men who had too much time on their hands. What was the expression? The devil has work for idle hands?

Now that the pawky pair had caught sight of the book, they were never going to leave him alone about it.

They returned within minutes, shut his door, and then settled into the chairs in front of his desk. Ronan poured each of them a glass of port. In truth, it was of excellent quality. He could tell by the deep crimson of the liquid.

It tasted smooth and sweet as it slid down his throat.

Ronan drained his glass and set it aside. "Robbie, do you realize what this means? Joshua has just found the leprechaun's pot of gold."

"What do ye mean?" He eyed the book curiously.

"The ladies have used it to trap unsuspecting bachelors into falling in love with them. Well, why can't we use it ourselves? Except not to find love, but to avoid their traps. Don't you see? Think of this as a battle of the sexes. This book contains their battle plans, their maps, their weapons. We only need to study this and be prepared to cut them off at every turn. Think of how easy it will be to thwart their plans if we know exactly what they are going to do and when they are going to do it?"

Robbie's eyes lit up. "Let's take it a step further. We can turn the game on them. Instead of them luring us into a parson's trap, we can lure them into our beds."

Joshua set his feet off the desk and rose with a frown. "Ruin innocents? This is your battle plan?"

"Och, no. We'll keep away from the unspoiled ones. But we all know that most of these debutantes have given up their petals. So what harm is there in aiming for the ones we want and going after them? Maybe two or three in one night? Maybe all three at once?"

Joshua sighed. "This is what you have in mind? To become stud bulls for the despoiled daughters of the aristocracy?"

Robbie laughed. "Are ye suggesting there is something wrong with that?"

He clenched his hands, not knowing why he was behaving like a prig at the moment. This had been their lives until now, fighting hard, drinking hard, and playing hard. They took women to their beds whenever they felt the need. Never a shortage of the cheaper sort who were not modest about their sexual desires. "This book is called *The Book of Love*. Not *The Book of Sex*. I don't know about you, but I would rather not spend the rest of my days falling into bed with women who mean nothing to me and might give me the pox."

Ronan shook his head. "Gad, don't tell me you're ready to marry. Have you found the girl?"

"No. I don't have anyone in mind. But I have no intention of passing her up when she does come along. When you infants finally grow up, you'll realize I'm right."

Robbie and Ronan began to leaf through the book again. "Love, ye say?" Robbie did not look convinced. "So, a slight modification to the battle plans. Instead of seeking out the ones who have given away their maidenheads, we look for the one jewel hidden among the crop of debutantes?"

"That's right. The one who will make you the perfect wife. This is what the author has been saying. The right girl for you doesn't have to be perfect for everyone, just for you. But you must also understand what it is you seek in your mate." He raked a hand through his hair, uncertain how much to tell them. But they now appeared to be listening intently, done with their little boy antics for the moment.

"How far along have you gotten into the book?" Ronan asked.

"About six or seven chapters." He hesitated to say more, but the pair suddenly looked seriously interested. "Do you want me to tell you what I've learned so far?"

They nodded.

"First, I must have your oaths that you will not damage this book or mock what is written in it."

Again nods.

"Say it."

Robbie went first. "I give ye my oath."

Ronan poured himself another glass of port. "I do, too. You have my oath." He refilled Joshua and Robbie's glasses. "Here's to learning about love." Then he grinned wickedly. "And to the many ladies who will lead us down the wrong paths of pleasure along the way."

"Bollocks, you're an idiot."

Robbie grinned as well. "Och, dinna scowl at us, Josh. Ye have no idea how insistent some of those lassies can be. Who are we to deny them? But we gave ye our oaths to learn about the true lass of our heart, so ye have our full attention. Go ahead. Tell us."

"Very well, here we go." He settled comfortably in his chair and started at the beginning. "Apparently, it is our brain that tells our heart what it ought to feel."

Ronan laughed. "I don't know about that. Most of the time, I think my brain shuts down when I see a room full of pretty girls. At first glance, I want them all."

"Och, aye. It is much the same for me," Robbie said with a nod. "And if they're eager, wouldn't it be cruel of me to deny them?"

"You're both still idiots but not exactly wrong in this. According to the author, men have two brains. A higher and a lower. One is complex, and the other simple."

It did not surprise Joshua when both of his companions made lewd remarks about their lower brains, gesturing to their crotches. He groaned silently. This was going to be a long afternoon.

He continued while Robbie refilled their glasses again. "The function of our lower brain is to have us find suitable sexual mates. So, the moment we see a female, that low brain immediately makes a quick assessment of her breeding qualities."

He ignored their snorts and more crass comments and gestures, merely rolling his eyes before continuing. "Is she too young? Too old? Too sickly? Too frail? This is what we consider in that instant. We look at her physical qualities, the shape of her body. Size of her breasts.

Breadth of her hips. We assess this before we move on to the color of her hair or eyes."

"I like a girl with big, robust breasts," Ronan remarked, holding out his hands and cupping them in the air. "A man needs something soft and meaty to hold on to."

"You could cup her arse," Robbie suggested, no doubt intending to be helpful, "if her breasts aren't big enough for you."

"The point of this chapter is to bring out the differences between male urges and female urges. We've been given two brains in order to seek out women capable of providing us with offspring, and then paring those choices down to find the right one for us."

"Why can't they all be right?" Ronan asked.

"Because if we bed them and leave them to breed, we also need to remain by their side to protect them. This is what the author says. We must remain to protect them or else they'll be eaten by wolves. Of course, he doesn't mean it literally. But a woman giving birth is probably at her most vulnerable at that time. Even for the next few years afterward. How is she to provide for her babes if she cannot leave them, and we are not there to provide for her? This is why we must use our higher brain function to select the one who will give us our heirs. She is the one we must stand by and protect."

Robbie groaned. "Ye're making me feel like a royal wretch. How am I to have fun if I'm to worry about every lass I bed?"

Ronan stood up. "I'm not ready for this. I agree with Robbie. It isn't as though that's all we do. How many years have we gone without while on the battlefield? Even now, we're usually kept too busy for more than an occasional tumble. But I'm going to have my fun while I can. We're careful in whom we choose to bed, aren't we? We take precautions. And no innocents are ruined."

Robbie rose along with him. "Och, aye. Ye ought to stop reading as well, Josh. The book isn't so much a battle plan as a battle trap, and ye're about to fall into it. I fear ye'll be married within the month if ye don't put that cursed thing down right now."

"I'm not putting it down. Don't you want to know about the five senses? Sight, taste, touch, scent, hearing? This is what the book explains. It's about really looking at someone and seeing them at their essence, not cluttering your mind with what you want to see or expect to see."

They left his office in a hurry.

So much for teaching them about love.

"Dumb arses," he muttered. "You're doomed no matter what you do."

Although he did not feel doomed so much as interested to know what love felt like. At this point in his life, he ought to be prepared to meet the right girl. He wanted to know what to look for and understand when something felt wrong.

He managed to finish the book now that his brother and Robbie were treating him as a leper. They had reason to pass his office several more times that afternoon but quickened their strides whenever walking by, as though he carried some sort of disease they might catch if they lingered too close by.

He called out to them when they passed by the fourth time. "Ronan! Robbie! Come in here."

They kept their heads down and hurried down the hall.

Cowards.

He rose from behind his desk and walked over to his window overlooking the Thames. The afternoon sun beat down upon the river so that the water took on a jeweled shimmer. The days were growing shorter now, and the sun was already beginning to sink on the horizon. The sky and clouds had taken on a pinkish hue.

He returned to Chipping Way, eager to prepare for Lord Milford's party. Were this a more formal affair, he would have dressed in black tie and civilian attire. But Lord Milford was high up in the War Ministry and would expect his officers to appear in dress uniform.

He had just walked out the door when Violet hurried over to him. "Oh, I'm so glad I caught you before you left. Uncle John wanted me to ask you if you'd like to ride with us. We're taking two carriages, and there's plenty of room."

"Thank you. I'd like that." He followed her next door, hoping to see Holly and know she had not made up an excuse to beg off.

There she was, just climbing into one of the carriages.

His heartbeat immediately quickened.

Rather annoying of his heart to behave this way now that he understood all that it meant. He'd obviously selected this young widow as one of his desirable breeding mates. Of course, she was off-limits to him for mere sport. If he ever took Holly to his bed, he would have to marry her.

Widow or not.

Experienced or not…well, she had to be experienced. Perhaps not adept at the sexual arts, but certainly no longer a virgin.

Not that it mattered. Holly could never be a dalliance for him.

But what were his feelings for her?

He was not particularly pleased to find himself riding with Holly. Not only riding with her but seated beside her as the Farthingale entourage rode to Lord Milford's home. He caught her lovely scent— honey and lavender. He felt the soft give of her body whenever she fell against him as the carriage bumped and rolled along the London streets.

Fortunately, Violet and Hortensia were in the seats opposite theirs. This once, he was relieved to stare into Hortensia's prune-faced scowl. By the mere arch of her eyebrow, she conveyed her threat. Touch one of my chicks, and I'll cleave you in half with a broadsword.

Violet was simply smiling at him, her expression also obvious. She wanted to match him with Holly. Indeed, she was giddy about it.

He glanced at Holly.

Her hands were tightly clasped and resting on her lap. Her head was bowed so that she was staring at everyone's feet.

She was dreading this party, already fretting about the dance he'd claimed. Well, he wasn't going to make it easier for her. He wasn't going to claim one dance, but two. First the waltz, then the supper dance. Then he was going to walk her into the dining hall and remain with her throughout the meal.

He wasn't certain why he needed to do this. But the more she wanted to hide, the more he was determined to drag her into the light.

They entered, were announced, and all headed to the ballroom, which was not nearly as large as those in the finer homes, but it easily held the one hundred or so guests invited. Holly darted straight over to the dowager countess, Lady Eloise Dayne, and sat down next to the elderly woman and her circle of gray-haired friends.

Damnation.

Lady Phoebe Withnall, London's most prolific gossip, now took a seat beside Holly. The two began to chat. Did Holly realize who this little termagant was? He wondered what secrets Lady Withnall meant to pry out of this lovely innocent.

Well, no. Holly wasn't innocent, precisely.

He shook his head, his instincts erring again. *Widow. Once married. Wedding night.* Perhaps many more nights with her husband.

Not that he cared.

Why should he care?

Ronan came up to him and clapped him on the shoulder. "Dead man walking."

"What?"

"Josh, if you stare at Violet's cousin any harder, you are going to burn a hole straight through her."

"That makes no sense. A look doesn't burn."

He calmly drank his glass of champagne. "I beg to differ. A fiery look will do just that. You are lit up like a torch. What's going on with the two of you?"

"Nothing."

Ronan clapped him on the shoulder again. "Right, why don't you tell that to Lady Miranda. She's headed straight for us. Ah, she's added henna to her hair again. Flame red this time."

"If you value your life, you won't remark on it. Bollocks, the last thing I need is our mother's meddling. Cut her off before she reaches me. Distract her," he said, beating a hasty retreat to the card room.

Robbie was seated at one of the card tables playing *vingt-un* with Joshua's brothers Finn and Tynan. He waved Joshua over. "Come join us. Fill yer brothers in on what ye've been doing."

"Shut up, Robbie." But he settled in the open chair.

"Good evening, tadpole," Tynan said, smirking at him. "Lady Miranda is looking for you."

He nodded. "I saw her coming and managed to avoid her. Why is she looking for me?"

Tynan shrugged. "I don't know."

Finn chuckled. "Perhaps a mother's sense that her baby boy needs her."

Tynan, Earl of Westcliff, was Joshua's eldest brother. Finn was the next. Then him. Ronan was the youngest of the four, but they were all fairly close in age. They were also all as tall as oak trees and had the muscular build of battle-hardened warriors. There was not a *baby boy* among them. In truth, he was amazed their mother had managed to survive delivering four sons the size of oxen.

Well, Lady Miranda was a force to be reckoned with in her own right. And while they all loved her dearly, she simply wasn't the quiet, sit by the fire and knit scarves, motherly sort.

No, indeed. They were all convinced she'd been Queen Boudica in a prior life, for no one could rampage, pillage, and burn through London as efficiently as her.

Joshua seemed to be having luck at cards even though his concentration was not what it ought to have been. He couldn't wait for the first dances to end to take his turn at the waltz with Holly.

The sight of her earlier, sitting amid the gray-haired, elderly widows still made his blood boil. She'd looked beautiful seated there, her hair loosely drawn back in an elegant coil and pinned at the nape of her neck. Her gown was another of those drab confections, but on her, the pale gray silk appeared luminescent. The simplicity of the gown only served to enhance her beautiful body.

At last, he collected his winnings and rose. "My apologies, gentlemen. Duty calls."

"This I have got to see," Robbie muttered, rising with him.

Finn and Tynan tossed aside their cards. "Who's the lucky girl, tadpole?" Tynan asked.

"Holly Farthingale," Robbie said.

Finn pounded him on the back. "When's the wedding?"

"There isn't going to be one. Just because you married Belle doesn't mean I must be next."

Finn ignored him and spoke to the others. "Belle knew it. She and her sister gave Holly that book. Just go with it, Josh. You don't stand a chance."

"Yes, he does," Robbie said. "Holly gave him the book."

Joshua let out a string of invectives. "So much for your vow of silence."

"What? I promised not to damage the book or mock what was written in it." He held up his hands as Joshua started toward him. "Stop, Josh! Where's the harm in telling your brothers? Isn't Finn the latest Brayden to fall because of that book? And I never promised to keep quiet about your having it. But I will now. My lips are sealed. I won't mention it again."

"Why did Holly give it to you?" Tynan asked, his gaze now thoughtful.

Joshua turned to Finn. "Did Belle say anything to you about it?"

"No, only that she and Honey were determined Holly should have it next. Why did she hand it off to you?"

"She didn't want it. I caught her trying to hide it. She stuffed it in my hands and told me I could read it if I wanted to. That's what I did this afternoon."

"And?" Finn appeared ready to burst into laughter.

He shrugged. "And nothing. It's only a damn book. I read it." He strode out of the gaming room and went in search of Holly. He'd last seen her with Lady Dayne and Lady Withnall. But she wasn't beside them now. Bloody, bloody hell. She and her sisters were standing with Sophie Farthingale, Finn's wife, Belle…and his mother.

The damn woman had a nose like a bloodhound.

He took a deep breath and strode over to them.

His mother cast him a broad smile. "Ah, here's my son now. But I believe you all know him, so introductions are unnecessary."

"Good evening, ladies." He dutifully bussed his mother's cheek.

She stared at him in silence as though waiting for him to say something more. *Ha!* He was keeping his mouth shut. But his gaze warned his mother to keep out of his affairs. She was staring back at him, in effect telling him to go stuff it and he'd better choose one of these Farthingales to marry before her hair turned gray, which it would never do because Lady Miranda was forever forty, had barrels of henna stocked in her cellar, and no son of hers had better comment on it if he wished to live to see tomorrow's sunrise.

He turned to Holly. "I believe this dance is mine."

Holly's cheeks turned to flame. "Is it? Are you certain?"

Wordlessly, he held out his arm to her.

She made no move to take it.

Everyone was staring at them, including Lady Withnall, who had the ears of a bat, the eyes of an eagle, and the instincts of a jungle cat hunting prey. She was headed straight for their little group, the *thuck, thuck, thuck* of her cane causing panic in everyone she passed.

Joshua took Holly's hand and placed it on his arm, keeping his own hand over hers on the chance she attempted to draw it away. "Miss Dahlia. Miss Heather. I shall see you later."

They giggled.

He led Holly onto the dance floor. One would think he was leading a lamb to slaughter. He sighed. "What's wrong?"

"I don't know how to waltz. It wasn't all the rage in our quieter social circle in York. I didn't think you were serious about claiming me for it. I haven't danced a single dance in over five years. Please, Joshua. Don't make me do this. Take me back to Aunt Sophie."

He sighed. "No, but come with me. I have another idea."

Her sparkling eyes widened in surprise. "What? Where are you taking me?"

"Onto the veranda. We'll dance there, out of everyone's way." He glanced at her, saw she was nibbling her lip and fretting. But her lower lip was plump and quivering in a manner he found surprisingly arousing and erotic.

"People will talk!"

"Let them. We'll only be dancing. Anyone can see us from the ballroom and know this is all we are doing."

"Promise me that's all we'll be doing."

"What more do you think I intend to do?" He noticed her chest was lightly heaving, and her gaze was on his lips. He cast her a wickedly lazy smile. "What more would you like me to do?"

CHAPTER FOUR

W*RETCHED MAN!*
Holly was not going to do anything with Joshua but dance. Wasn't this bad enough? Her knees were knocking, and her entire body was shaking as he led her onto the veranda.

"Is it too cold for you, Holly?"

The veranda was sheltered from the cool breeze, and without the wind to cut through her bones, she was fairly comfortable. Not to mention the heat radiating off Joshua's body had somehow found its way into her blood, causing it to bubble like a pool of lava. "No, I'm fine."

He looked so big and splendid in his uniform, he made her wits scatter. She was going to melt in his arms if she wasn't careful.

He smiled at her. "Relax. I am not about to toss you off a cliff."

Perhaps not, but she still felt as though she were falling. Tumbling. Reeling.

Was it a sin to want to be held close and made to feel special tonight? This is what she'd wanted to do, wanted to feel ever since meeting Joshua.

The butterflies in her stomach began to flutter, just as they had last night when he'd stood before her in his bronzed glory.

Apparently, he affected her in the same dizzying way whether he wore clothes or not.

Oh, drat.

She had finally managed to scrub away the vision of him emerging naked from his bath, and now it had popped right back into her head.

He cupped her chin and raised her gaze to his, still smiling as he regained her attention. "Put your hand on my shoulder."

"Like this?" She must have done it right because her entire body was now tingling. Oh, good gracious, his shoulder felt so good beneath her palm.

"Perfect," he said with a raspy softness, placing his hand on her waist to draw her closer. He took her other hand, gently clasped it in his, and held it out so that they were now in the proper stance. "When I move forward, you'll take a step back. Just follow the flow of my body, and let my hand at your waist guide you. Shall we give it a try?"

"Yes, I'm ready." She stared at their feet.

"Look up at me, Holly."

She dared not, but he was insistent. When she finally did, she almost swooned in response to his devastatingly tender smile. "You look beautiful by moonlight."

She shook her head. "That's because you cannot see me clearly."

"I can see you perfectly. I think you're the one who refuses to see who you really are." But he gave her no time to protest before he began to lead her through the steps with unexpectedly fluid grace.

She felt as though she were floating on a cloud.

"That's it, just look at me. Remember to let your body move with mine."

This. This is how it should have been with Walter and never was. He'd never transported her to magical heights. True, they'd never danced the waltz or ever danced after they were married. But taking this lesson with Joshua made her realize that not everything wrong in the marriage had been her fault.

Walter had to share in the blame. They'd attended many parties after they were wed. He'd never indulged in a dance with her. Usually, he went off with one or two of his closest friends, only to appear later to escort her into supper. It was not long into their marriage before he no longer did even that.

The realization upset her, causing her to accidentally stumble over Joshua's booted foot. "I'm sorry."

"Don't apologize to me, Holly. You're doing beautifully."

She glanced at her toes before raising her gaze to his once more. "I am?"

He nodded. "Close your eyes if it feels easier to follow the movement of my body without looking at me."

She fluttered them closed.

"It is easier," she said with some surprise. "This is amazing. Even though I cannot see you, I can feel the subtle changes in your body. It's as though we are connected, soaring together, our feet no longer touching the ground." She gasped. "I didn't mean—"

"I know what you mean. When you turn off one sense, that of sight, the other senses seem to take over, don't they? Now your sense of *us* is heightened. You can tell by the merest touch of my hand that we're about to turn, and now follow me as I take a step back."

"This is wonderful, Joshua. Thank you." Her eyes were still closed, and she was taking in each glorious sensation. She breathed him in, loving the sandalwood scent of his skin. Tingles shot through her whenever he spoke, for his voice was deep and resonant.

His touch burned through the silk of her gown.

His lips were whisper-soft against her ear, and she thought she would expire on the spot when he accidentally grazed her cheek.

Perhaps not an accident.

Was it possible he enjoyed touching her?

"You are most welcome, Holly."

Was it possible this dance was as thrilling for him as it was for her? He did not seem at all bored. Not that she could be sure, for she really knew nothing about men. But he made her feel as though his time with her was something special.

As she became more proficient, he quickened their pace. "Look at that, you were born to dance."

She opened her eyes and laughed. "What rubbish. But thank you again. I'm having fun."

She cast him a warm smile, one he could barely see under the moon's glow, and yet she thought she heard his breath hitch. "Finally," he said in a husky murmur that sent more tingles shooting through her. "A genuine smile out of you."

Perhaps he had been able to see her, after all. He had the keen eyes of a trained soldier. In addition to moonlight, there was a little candlelight filtering out from the ballroom and some more from the lit torches lining the garden paths. But they were distant and faint.

She was happy, and she hadn't felt this way in a very long time. Indeed, in so long a time, she'd forgotten how to laugh.

When the music finally came to an end, she hesitated to let him go. He felt so solid and divine. How many times had she thanked him? She'd lost count. But as he was about to release her, she thanked him again. "I cannot remember having quite so much fun ever. I hope I wasn't too awful."

His eyes seemed to absorb her, seemed to draw her in, and drag her under like a dangerous whirlpool. Was he going to kiss her?

Please, kiss me.

She knew very well he couldn't since they were in sight of the ballroom. They must have provided amusement for at least a dozen guests who were seated by the doors.

"Holly." His voice was as smooth as melted chocolate, his gaze smoldering. "I want you to close your eyes another moment."

She inhaled lightly. "Are you going to kiss me? You can't while everyone is watching."

"I know. I'm not going to kiss you. Close your eyes."

"What are you going to do?" Her heart was beating so fast, she could hardly breathe. But she obeyed him, hoping he would toss caution to the wind and seek her lips.

He ran his thumb gently across her lower lip. Then he slowly traced it along the curve of her mouth. "I know it isn't the same as a kiss."

No, but it felt divine. Almost as though his mouth was on hers. She'd never been touched like this before.

"Blessed saints, you're so beautiful." His whispered words sounded reverent, as though spoken in wonder. "I'm going to kiss you if we stay out here a moment longer. I had better take you inside. Save the supper dance for me."

She opened her eyes, not bothering to hide her surprise. "You want a second dance with me?" If he did not stop being nice to her, she was going to fall in love with him. Oh, this was a disaster. She couldn't allow it.

He raked a hand raggedly through his hair. "I would claim a dozen dances with you if I could," he said with a pained laugh.

Oh, heavens!

This was not him speaking.

"Oh, dear. Joshua, I know what this is. You've read that book, haven't you? And now you think you're feeling something for me. But it is only because I was the one who gave the book to you."

"I have read it," he said with a nod. "Now that I have, I'm more convinced than ever you ought to read it, too."

She eased out of his grasp. "I won't."

"Fine, keep on hiding. But you need not worry about my feelings. I have no intention of giving my heart to the wrong girl." He led her back to her Aunt Sophie. "Until the supper dance."

She stared at his back as he walked away.

And died a little inside when he claimed Dahlia for the next dance.

Despite having waltzed in the outdoor chill, her body felt overheated. Since her aunt was busy chatting with friends, she moved away unnoticed and walked over to the punch bowl. She was waiting for those ahead of her to move on when someone called her name.

She turned, and the color drained from her face. "Mr. Gleason. Mrs. Gleason. I...I hadn't realized you were in London. When did you get in? Where are you staying?"

"Do you often dance outdoors with uniformed soldiers?" Mrs. Gleason intoned, her disapproval obvious.

But this is how it had always been with Walter's parents. They'd disapproved of their son marrying her. They'd disapproved of the way she ran his household. Most hurtful of all, they'd quickly cut ties with her, asking her to leave their marital abode even before his body had turned cold in the grave. They owned the house, not Walter.

"Captain Brayden is family. He was kind enough to teach me how to waltz. I didn't know how since Walter never saw fit to dance with me."

Walter's father frowned at her. "Ah, I see nothing has changed. Still blaming our son for your failures as a dutiful wife."

She tipped her chin up, trying to maintain her dignity. "Well, it has been lovely running into you again. I see my aunt is summoning me. If you will excuse me."

She hurried back to the safety of the Farthingale fold, still thirsty. Still aching to be held in Joshua's arms. But her one moment of beauty had been shattered by Walter's parents. Could they not let her forget how badly she'd failed their son?

She felt herself about to burst into tears but had too much pride to allow anyone to see her cry. There were only a few people on the veranda. She didn't wish to be seen by them either, but surely no one was in the garden. She could hide there while she cried.

That's all she needed, a quick burst of tears, and then she'd be all right again. Well, never all right. But sufficiently composed so that she could return to the party with no one the wiser. Even if someone noticed her red eyes, she could always blame it on someone's perfume.

She tried not to run out but merely walked with purpose onto the veranda. Several couples were out there. No one bothered to pay her any attention. The wind bit her cheeks when she walked out of the shelter of the veranda and fled down the steps to lose herself in the garden. In truth, it was cold outside.

But she wasn't ready to turn back.

She sank onto a stone bench beside a row of boxwood, buried her face in her hands, and cried. She was so unhappy, but didn't want to hide away like this any longer. Joshua was right in telling her she ought to read *The Book of Love*. She didn't want all the beauty in life to pass her by. Nor did she want to be prune-faced, watching everyone get on with their lives while she sat alone and continued to blame herself for failing as a wife.

Perhaps the Gleasons had done her a favor by insulting her.

Indeed, this had been the pattern of her marriage to Walter, them always finding fault, and Walter doing nothing to stop them. He'd never stood by her. She'd been too young then, not even eighteen when first married, and not strong enough to fight for herself.

Yet too ashamed to ever turn to her parents for help.

As she cried, she felt the presence of someone else now kneeling beside her. "Holly, who were those people? What did they say to you?"

"Oh, Joshua!" She threw her arms around his neck, not thinking about what she was doing, only knowing that she needed to hold onto him or else she'd drown in the sea of her sorrows.

He wrapped his arms around her and drew her up with him, pressing her body against the heat and hardness of his. He caressed her cheek and ran his hands up and down her shivering arms.

"How did you know I was out here? You were dancing with my sister. The music hasn't ended."

"Do you think I cared? Dahlia saw you walk out as well. She understood I had to come after you. Who are those people?"

"Walter's parents. The Gleasons. They've never forgiven me for chasing their son away. They think I made him so unhappy, he ran off to war because he could no longer stand to live with me. It isn't true, Joshua."

"I know."

"You believe me?"

He nodded.

"I think he went off to fight because his closest friends had done so only a week before he enlisted. He didn't run off because of me. I was inconsequential to him. I don't know why he married me. He never loved me."

"Then, he was a monumental fool."

She sniffled against his chest, her cheek resting against the light wool of his jacket. "I was the fool."

"No, you were too young to know any better. He used you, although I don't know for what purpose."

She continued to cling to him because she still felt as though she might drown if she ever let go. "I don't want to die old and unhappy. But I don't know how to change myself. I'm no longer a silly eighteen-year-old. I cannot bat my lashes and flirt and giggle inanely."

"No, you can only be yourself." He kissed the top of her head.

"But who am I, Joshua? I don't recognize myself anymore. How do I find myself again?"

He kissed her cheek and must have felt the wetness of her tears against his lips. He drew away slightly and ran his thumb along her cheek to wipe away the teardrops. "Holly, that book you gave me..."

"No, I don't want it back yet. I'm still afraid."

"Why?"

"My mind is too cluttered to make sense of my feelings. I've heard my cousins speak of it. It's quite powerful. I don't know what it will do to me."

He feathered light kisses on her eyes. "I have a proposition for you. I've read it. Let me guide you through it. Will you agree to this? If a passage proves too difficult, we'll skip over it. Perhaps return to it later when you are more confident."

"But this book is about understanding and finding true love. How can you be sure you've got it right yourself? Have you ever been in love?"

"No." He caressed her cheek again. "But I know love when I see it. And I know how others have cruelly twisted you into believing you are undeserving of it. What do you say? Will you do this with me?"

She nibbled her lip, about to refuse because being too close to Joshua frightened her. But here they were already alone in a dark garden. She was wrapped in his arms, clinging to him with desperation.

Perhaps falling in love with him.

But how could she trust her feelings?

This uncertainty was all the more reason she had to get love right. "Yes, Joshua. I will."

He released the breath he must have been holding.

Had her answer mattered to him?

He withdrew his handkerchief and used it to dry her eyes. She laughed. "I'll owe you another handkerchief. That's two I've taken from you."

"I have another dozen at the ready for you."

"No, I think two must be my limit. I've cried enough tears to last me a good long while. I'm tired of being a watering pot. And tired of hiding myself away."

"Hurrah! Good for you, Holly."

"How are we to do this? You spend your days in Parliament. We're often busy in the evenings. I can't very well come to you in the wee hours of the morning."

"I promise to keep my shirt and trousers on if you do."

She laughed, although it sounded much like a groan. "Out of the question."

"Out of the question that I keep my clothes on? Or out of the question that I take them off?"

"Kindly be serious. This is important to me."

"You're right. Sorry. You're easy to tease. Can you visit me at my office? Not alone, of course. I don't think Violet or your sisters would mind accompanying you. My brother Ronan is also assigned there. So is Robert MacLauren. Violet knows both of them. They'll entertain Violet and your sisters while we read. How does that sound?"

"A workable plan. I'll ask them tonight. If they're agreeable, we'll come by tomorrow in the early afternoon. Is that all right?"

"More than all right. You're shivering. Let's get you back inside before you make yourself ill. In any event, we'd better return before anyone notices we're both missing. The music has stopped."

"Oh, then we had better go in separately."

He nodded. "You go in first. I'll stand out here for a while. But I'm still claiming you for the supper dance, and then I'll escort you to supper."

She could not hide her surprise. "Are you not tired of me yet?"

"No, Holly. Not even the littlest bit."

She walked in, shaking her head, wanting to understand how a man like Joshua could be so kind and patient with her. Perhaps that book would explain it because she had no answers. All she knew was that he made her feel young and alive again.

Well, she was still young. Only two and twenty years of age. But until now, she'd carried herself as though she were a widow of two and sixty years.

No longer.

No more wearing these dull-colored gowns. She'd borrow cheerier gowns from her sisters and cousins if she had to since they were all of similar size and height. They would require little alteration.

More importantly, she would no longer hide in corners.

Joshua had feathered kisses on her face, but he hadn't really *kissed* her yet. *Yet?* Was this what she wanted? If she was to be honest about it, yes. He'd had the perfect opportunity to kiss her romantically when they were alone in the garden.

Had the thought crossed his mind?

Perhaps he didn't want to.

Well, it was for the best he hadn't. She did not want to be kissed out of curiosity or pity. When Joshua kissed her, she wanted it to be because he loved her.

Perhaps she was hoping for too much.

But was it wrong of her to hold out for the chance of love?

CHAPTER FIVE

J OSHUA REMAINED STANDING alone in the garden for another few minutes. The next dance had started, but he was in no hurry to join in the revelry. He needed the enveloping night breeze to cool his ardor and allow him to regain control of himself.

Holly.

This young widow tore at his heart. He'd wanted to crush his mouth to hers and kiss her into oblivion. But how could he? She was too distraught, so confused and vulnerable. If he had kissed her, she would have surrendered to him completely.

He could have taken full advantage.

But this was not the Brayden way.

No matter how much he wanted to nibble the sensitive pulse at the base of her throat or lick along her soft lips, he could not do it.

Not yet.

But Lord help him! He was counting the hours, the minutes before he would do just that, and more.

That he would kiss her eventually was not in question. Only the timing of it remained in doubt. Nor did he doubt he would seek more from Holly, for her body, even hidden under those drab gowns she wore, had him in spasms.

He was not used to these conflicting urges warring inside of him. Until Holly, his choices had been easy. Keep away from the innocent lasses. Bed the willing ones. Move on. No promises. No complications.

But Holly?

She was the definition of the word *complication*.

He could not bed her unless he was willing to marry her. Even if he found the strength within himself to keep his hands off her, how could he move on? There was an innocent quality to her beauty that he simply could not resist. She drew him to her like a moth to a flame.

Her eyes. Her smile. Her sweetness and vulnerability. Her hurt.

Yet, she was not weak.

There was a quiet strength in her that only needed the right guidance to be drawn out. He meant to be the one to guide her. But what then? Could he let her go?

Did he want to let her go?

In truth, he didn't think so.

He strolled back inside and remained standing alone on the periphery of the ballroom, watching her as she joined her sisters in chatting with friends and potential beaus. He kept a sharp watch, ready to interfere if any man appeared too interested in her.

While he was not yet certain what to do about her, he was not ready to allow another man near her. He could pretend the reason was to protect her from scoundrels, but mostly it was because he was a possessive, low-brain arse.

What did she mean to him?

The thought plagued him, but he did not have to figure it out tonight.

Since Ronan and Robbie were chatting with her and her sisters, he knew Holly was in safe company. But the moment the others moved off to dance the next set, Holly was suddenly left standing alone.

The Gleasons, like the jackals they were, descended upon her again.

Joshua immediately tensed.

They had yet to speak to Holly, and her face had already turned ashen.

He walked over in time to hear them mention something about a ring. "...you know it belongs in our family. You are no longer a part of it," was the tail end of what he heard.

"Is there a problem, Miss Far...Mrs. Gleason?" he corrected, realizing he'd never thought of her as married to another man. To him, she was Holly Farthingale.

She looked as though she wanted the floor to open up and suck her in. "No, Captain Brayden. Thank you." She sighed when he did not move away. "There seems to be a misunderstanding about a ring."

"Which belongs to us," Mr. Gleason intoned, his expression dark and challenging. His wife's expression was merely icy, not a trace of warmth in her eyes or her pinched lips.

Joshua stared at Holly, knowing this goodhearted girl would never keep something that did not belong to her. This was just her late husband's family seeking to hurt her again.

"It was my bride token," Holly explained. "Walter gave it to me on our wedding day. He never said anything about it belonging to his family. I thought he'd bought it for me."

Joshua folded his arms across his chest. "I'm sure he did."

Mr. Gleason's anger turned on him. "Are you calling us liars?"

"I am merely questioning why it has taken you years to ask for it back. Did it not occur to you to ask for it or at least mention its significance, when you kicked Mrs. Gleason out of her home? You certainly had the presence of mind to do that within a week of her husband's burial."

"The ring is ours, whether it is a family heirloom or not," said Mr. Gleason. "Our son had no funds of his own. Everything he had was provided by me. If he purchased the ring, it was done with my blunt. I own it."

Joshua wanted to grab these interlopers by the scruff of their necks and toss them into the street. They were making up this latest claim in order to hurt Holly. Their son had obviously given the ring to her as a bride token, just as she'd said. Whether a court of law would require her to return it was doubtful.

Holly placed a hand on his arm. "Thank you, Captain Brayden. But I don't want it. They had only to ask for it years ago, and I would have given it to them. But just to be clear, Walter did purchase it for me. He told me the name of the jeweler's shop where he acquired it. As far as I know, they are still in business. It would be a simple matter to get at the truth."

Walter's parents appeared nonplussed. "Keep it, if it means that much to you," the mother said. "We know you care more for it than you ever did for our son."

Holly's hand was still on his arm, and he felt it trembling. "Where are you staying? I shall have one of the Farthingale footmen deliver it to you tomorrow. But I ask that you give him a receipt for it in return. I wouldn't want any further misunderstandings."

"We're lodging at the Highmore," said Mr. Gleason. "Have him bring it over tomorrow morning at ten o'clock."

Joshua did not want them causing any more mischief. "I have a better idea. I'm good friends with the Royal Navy's liaison to Parliament. He owes me a favor. The Highmore is along his way to the Admiralty offices. I shall ask him to deliver the ring to you. If you still have a complaint, you may lodge it with the Admiralty."

The pair walked away displeased and a little intimidated.

Holly turned to him, burying her face against his arm as she laughingly snorted. "Royal Navy liaison? That's your brother Ronan."

He grinned. "I thought it sounded more impressive. I don't want Sophie and John getting mixed up in this meanspirited nonsense. That conniving pair would have accused the poor footman of delivering a fake, or some such rot. I saw the scheme in Gleason's eyes. They won't dare accuse an officer in the Royal Navy. Ronan can appear quite fierce and daunting when he isn't being an idiot."

"I'll be glad never to see them again. I don't care about the ring. I know they asked for it, thinking it would hurt me. But why should I hold on to anything from that family? Their son did not love me. I've hidden the truth from everyone, including myself."

"What they did to you is inexcusable." His grin faded. "I'm more determined than ever to see you free of their taint. It's time for the real Holly Farthingale to be allowed to shine. We start on this project tomorrow."

She nodded. "I'm looking forward to it with all my heart."

"I know." Because this girl had a big, loving heart that until this moment, had been stepped on, kicked, and battered. "Let me find Ronan before he slips away. I'll let him know to stop by Chipping Way tomorrow morning."

"Thank you. It feels good to have someone on my side."

"Always, Holly." He wanted to take her in his arms, but when did he not? "I owe your sister this next dance. Will you be all right if I leave you?"

"Yes, I see my cousin Dillie by the punch bowl. I'll stay with her until they call the supper dance…that is, if you still wish to dance with me. I know I've already asked you this, but I seem to be causing you an awful lot of trouble this evening. I would completely understand if—"

"No trouble at all. Yes, I'll come back to claim you for the supper dance." He walked her over to her cousin, relieved to see Dillie's husband, the Duke of Edgeware, with her. No one would dare approach Holly while under this duke's watch.

He then spoke to Ronan, whose eyes lit up at the prospect of the assignment. "I ought to be the one thanking Holly for the chance to relieve my boredom. Of course, I'll gladly do it."

"Don't start a fight with the oaf. Holly just wants them out of her life." He walked over to Holly's sister to claim the dance he'd promised her.

Heather was all giggles as he twirled her around the floor, but he didn't mind nearly as much as he usually did when dancing with these younger debutantes. She was only eighteen and therefore permitted to be lighthearted and frivolous.

But he could not help noticing the stark contrast between the two sisters. Heather was a happily innocent debutante, asking him questions about the various noblemen at the party. "Is he a rake? A scoundrel? Worthy husband material?"

He warned her away from most of the men she'd pointed out.

In contrast, Holly had already been married at that age and was having the confidence trounced out of her by her husband and his poisonous parents.

It seemed forever, but could not have been more than half an hour before the supper dance was called. Holly, in her pale gray silk gown, looked like an angel, lovelier than all the other young ladies in the crowd.

She knew this lively reel, apparently.

When the music started, although she was still her reserved self, he felt the excitement coursing through her body. There was no doubt she was enjoying the dance immensely. He was pleasantly surprised when she even managed to flirt with him, batting her eyelashes at him and casting him a fetching smile or two amid their hops, skips, and turns.

If she teased him like this when meeting at his office tomorrow, he'd draw the shades, barricade his door, and have his lustful way with her.

She was devastating to his senses.

He couldn't touch her or look at her without his body turning to fire. When she laughed, genuinely laughed, she filled the empty recesses of his heart.

Him?

He'd long outgrown his lovesick schoolboy urges.

After the dance, he escorted her into supper. Lord Milford's tables were laden to groaning with an impressive assortment of game fowl, venison, and fish, some cooked in their own juices and some basted with plum or apricot glazes.

He picked the choicest morsels and made a plate for her.

She ate like a bird, but he was used to eating like a Brayden, which meant loading a side of beef on a plate and using his fork as a weapon to ward off his brothers and cousins if they attempted to steal it away. "Too much?"

Holly laughed. "I would say so. This plate weighs more than I do. Have some, Joshua. I'm sure this is a mere appetizer portion for you. How did you and your brothers not eat your parents out of hearth and home?"

He arched an eyebrow. "I have no idea. Mealtime often resembled a cage of lions fighting over slabs of raw meat."

"That's how you became known as the wildebeests. Finn told us. But he also said that among yourselves, you also had pet names." She gave a merry laugh. "You, Finn, Ronan, and Romulus were known as the tadpoles. Is this true?"

"Yes. Caleb was the squid. Silly, I know. We call each other that when we want to rile each other, but in a friendly way. We've always been close. A few tussles, but never anything serious."

"And what of your older cousins?"

"The earls? No, they're just Tynan, James, and Marcus. They were too big for us to tease back then. If we tried, they'd just knock us on our arses."

"I love that your family is close and that you band together to protect each other. I like the way you came to my rescue with the Gleasons."

"I think you could have handled them."

She pursed her lips. "I don't know. Perhaps, but I think not yet. In time. It is surprisingly hard to shake that sick-to-one's-stomach feeling I get whenever I see them. They've always affected me this way. I wanted to tell them to go stuff it, but my stomach was roiling, and my body began to tremble. It was all I could do to keep from tossing up my accounts."

"We'll work on this tomorrow. I'll turn you into a Roman general yet."

She shook her head and laughed again. "Yes, I'd like that."

He enjoyed the sound of her merry lilt. He loved the sparkle in her eyes, and the gentle smiles she bestowed on him. Most importantly, he loved the trust she'd placed in him. She had let her guard down and was showing him the Holly she used to be.

They lingered over their plates, moving on to the Viennese desserts set out on tables at the opposite side of the dining hall. By the time they'd finished, they were among the last to quit the hall.

Joshua escorted her into the ballroom.

Holly turned pensive again, he could tell by the little droop at the corners of her mouth that made her look sensual and pouting. "Thank you for a lovely time, Joshua."

"Are you through with me already?"

She looked up at him in surprise. "No, but I thought…that is…are there not other women who have claim to your attention? As for me, you are the only one who has given me any notice. But I much prefer quality to quantity. One of you is worth a dozen of anyone else."

He grinned. "There's no one else for me. I only asked your sisters to dance because I did not want to be obvious about my wanting to claim two turns with you. But I doubt I've fooled anyone. When I wasn't dancing with you, I was staring at you."

"Really?" Her eyes widened in surprise.

He nodded.

She cleared her throat. "Joshua, may I ask you a question?"

"Of course." They had crossed the ballroom and were standing together beside the doors leading onto the veranda where they'd waltzed earlier.

"I was quite overset after seeing the Gleasons, so perhaps this is why you did not…"

"Why I did not, what?"

"I was curious as to why you did not kiss me romantically when we were alone in the garden? You kissed my brow, my cheek. You did nothing more. I'm so sorry, I know this question must sound extremely rude. It's just that I no longer trust my instincts. I no longer know what to think or feel. I was sure you were going to kiss me…on the lips. But you didn't."

Blessed saints.

"It wasn't from lack of wanting to, Holly. But you were too vulnerable. I don't think you would have stopped me."

"I wouldn't have," she admitted. "In that moment, you were my knight in shining armor. You overwhelmed me with your honor and valor."

"This is why I did not kiss you. What I felt for you in that moment was neither honorable nor valiant. I didn't trust myself to stop at just one kiss."

"You would have given me two kisses?"

He raked a hand through his hair. "You will slap me if I tell you what I would have done to you."

"No, I won't."

He shook his head and laughed. "Yes, indeed you will."

She regarded him, confused. "Three kisses?"

Did this girl not understand male urges? Had her husband never—

He shook his head, unable to conceive of the thought. No. Not possible. Had her husband not desired her?

If he ever had Holly in his bed, he would be a wild, untamed thing. A rutting boar, unreservedly kissing and touching her in every way possible. Tasting her creamy skin. Burying himself inside her.

He stared at her, equally confused.

Was it possible her husband had never once touched her?

CHAPTER SIX

HOLLY BORROWED ONE of Dahlia's gowns to wear for their afternoon visit to the Houses of Parliament. No more widow's weeds. Her sisters and Violet all felt it important to share their opinions. "You look stunning," Dahlia said, smiling in approval.

"Beautiful," Heather added.

"Joshua's jaw is going to drop to the floor when he sees you," Violet said with a merry laugh.

"I'm not..." She gave up the pretense, for they all knew she liked Joshua. Sighing, she gave herself a last look in the mirror before they left. She wore an ivory muslin with azure trim at the collar and hem, and pink and lavender floral bouquets embroidered throughout.

She hardly recognized herself. The gown was light and frivolous, and nothing like those she had worn these past five years. The azure trim brought out the blue in her eyes. The pink flowers brought out the natural blush in her cheeks. As for the lavender, it simply suited her complexion.

She hoped Joshua would like it.

"Holly's in love," her sisters teased, keeping up the irritating refrain as their carriage rolled along the London streets.

She turned in exasperation to Violet. "They won't listen to me. Do tell them to stop their ridiculous chant. I am not in love with Joshua."

Which only brought on giggles and a renewal of their refrain, "Holly's in love."

Violet was no help. "Are you certain you don't find him the handsomest man in existence? Because I can attest to the fact that there is nothing more delicious than these Brayden men. I have one of my own, and I love him fiercely. I'm sure Belle will say the same about Finn. They are smart, kind, protective, not to mention handsome as sin."

Holly did find Joshua to be all that. Good heavens, there wasn't a handsomer man alive. Her heart did flip-flops whenever he smiled at her. Last night at Lord Milford's had been an evening in paradise for her. Not even the Gleasons had been able to tarnish her pleasure. She'd danced with Joshua. He'd kissed her brow and cheek. He'd held her in his arms, the embrace so tender and protective, she was still reeling from the giddy splendor of it.

To have this forever would be a dream come true.

But she dared not think beyond today.

She dared not give her heart to him yet. It was too soon. Too fast. What of his feelings? Walter had tricked her into believing he loved her, but it hadn't been hard to fool a seventeen-year-old girl. With Joshua, it was different. First of all, she was different. She was no longer the naïve girl.

Yes, she was still unsure of herself and had no experience with men. But she hoped she was wise enough not to be tricked into another loveless marriage.

However, Joshua was nothing like Walter.

Joshua was a man. Walter, despite being in his early twenties when they'd wed, had always been a little boy. He'd lied to her and used her, although she did not understand to what purpose. He had not mistreated her. But why marry her if he wanted nothing to do with her?

"Here we are," Violet said.

"Oh, yes." Holly shook out of her thoughts.

Joshua came down to greet them and gave them a quick tour of the presently empty chambers in the House of Lords and House of Commons. He then led them upstairs to the topmost floor where the liaison offices were situated.

"Robert MacLauren and Ronan also have offices in this same wing of the building. They're at the north end of the hall. I'll take you there now. My office is at the south end."

"Is there a reason your offices are on opposite sides?" Dahlia asked.

"Army and navy?" Joshua laughed. "We are better kept apart. We're constantly fighting over the block of funds allotted to the military. As for the Scots, they had to be stuck somewhere, and there happened to be a vacant office near the navy liaison office. Robbie has the hardest job, I think. He has to fight for every leftover scrap to be given to the Scottish dragoon forces."

Holly could listen to him for hours. "This is so interesting, Joshua. What is it like when Parliament is in session?"

"Hectic, but far better than sitting on our hands and doing nothing. When in session, our primary duty is to present our budgets. These take months to prepare. The liaison officers do little of the actual budget preparation, but we have to know every detail of what goes in it."

"Why must you know every detail?" Dahlia asked.

"Because we are the ones who must convince the politicians to free up the purse strings. We are in constant meetings with the political parties, often with the prime minister and cabinet ministers. My role is to explain the army proposals, describe our latest military innovations. It isn't enough to assure them the innovations work. We have to be prepared to explain in detail how they work."

Holly pursed her lips in thought. "Does that not require a background in the sciences?"

"Yes, but we all have it. Me, Ronan, Robbie. Physics. Chemistry. Even ironworking. Diplomacy is a must. We constantly have to fight for funds for research and for procuring proper equipment and supplies for our soldiers. Ronan does the same for the navy. Robbie does the same for the Scots." He shook his head and sighed. "But there isn't one of us who would not rather be on a battlefield."

"Isn't that dangerous?" Heather asked.

"Yes, but it serves an immediate and useful purpose. On a field of battle, we are a band of brothers, if I may steal that description from Shakespeare's *Henry V*. In the Houses of Parliament? It's each politician for himself. I can see it in their eyes whenever we sit in these endless meetings. Some are quite decent men, of course. But others? They'll leave our soldiers without boots or coats if blocking the funds will serve their insignificant purposes."

Ronan came out of his office to greet them, soon followed by Robbie.

"We're all grateful for your visit," Ronan said. "It's a relief from our boredom. Oh, Holly, before I forget. Here's the receipt for you. I delivered that ring this morning."

"What ring?" Dahlia asked.

"One that Walter had given me, but I gave it to the Gleasons as a remembrance of their son." She tucked the receipt in her reticule and smiled at Ronan. "Thank you."

"I had a most pleasant conversation with them," he said with obvious sarcasm, arching a dark eyebrow. "They won't trouble you again."

Joshua quickly changed the topic of conversation before her sisters could ask more questions about the Gleasons. "Robbie and Ronan have taken to staging mock jousts with some of the other bored clerks. A tame affair so far, but it shall be livelier now that they have you fair damsels to favor them with their tokens."

Heather and Dahlia cheered.

Violet rolled her eyes but went along with the game.

Joshua took Holly's arm. "Let's leave them to their jousting." He led her down the hall to his office. "By the way, you look lovely. New gown?"

"Borrowed from Dahlia." She winced as she shook her head. "The gray silk I wore last night is the liveliest gown I own. I hadn't realized quite how badly I'd faded. I think this is the best word to describe what I've become. A mere shadow of my former self."

"We're going to fix that. Starting now." He led her into his office. She was surprised by its splendid view. But this was an advantage to being on the topmost floor. He had a spectacular view of the Thames and all of London that lay across the river.

He shut the door and turned to face her. "I know it isn't appropriate, but no one else is here to remark upon it, and I don't want us to be disturbed."

He motioned to a chair beside his desk, then surprised her by moving his chair out from behind the desk and setting it beside hers. "*The Book of Love* is safe at Violet's house. I didn't think we'd need it today. I thought we'd simply talk."

She nodded. "Whatever you think best."

He smiled at her, one of those tender smiles that melted her bones. "That book is about finding love. But first, I think you have to find yourself."

"Yes, it is a good way to describe what I need to do. But where to begin?"

He rubbed a hand across the nape of his neck. "You won't like this, but I think it all begins with Walter Gleason, doesn't it?"

She blushed. "I suppose."

"I know this is asking much of you, but will you tell me how you met and married him? How long were you married before he died? Obviously, it was not a happy arrangement. I'm not sure why you shouldered all the blame for it. There were two of you in the marriage." He took her hand and wrapped it in both of his. "I know these are deeply personal questions. I promise you, I'll keep whatever you tell me in confidence."

A chill ran through her, but his hands were big and warm, and she liked the way they enveloped hers. "I've never spoken about this to anyone, not even my parents. Certainly not my sisters. They're happy and looking forward to their debut season. I didn't want to dampen their excitement."

"I understand. Sometimes it is hardest to confide in your family."

She nodded. "I love them all dearly, but this is how I've felt all these years. They are too close to me. After Walter died, I didn't really want their opinions. Nothing they could say was going to bring him back." She took a deep breath, and with it took a leap of faith to trust Joshua, for how well did she really know him?

But she had to start trusting again, and she did feel safe and protected whenever she was with him. "The truth of it is," she said, "I was relieved when he left me to enlist in the army."

She paused, waiting for him to respond to her admission.

But he said nothing, and she noticed no disapproval in his expression, so she continued. "I didn't want him back. Not that I wished him dead, either. I didn't at all. He was not a bad man. But I had no life with him. Not even in those first days of our marriage."

Joshua frowned. "What do you mean?"

Oh, no.

Had she said too much? It was one thing to reveal they were not happily married. But to provide specific details? "Never mind. It isn't important."

"Blessed saints!" His eyes widened, and he stared at her with open mouth. "Holly, did you ever have a wedding night?"

She tried to hide her anguish, but Joshua had a way of seeing straight to her heart. She slipped out of his grasp and shot to her feet. "I have to go. This is a dreadful mistake."

He rose along with her and placed his hands on her shoulders. "Stay. Don't hide from the truth. Who are you hurting but yourself?"

"Fine, then I'm only hurting myself."

"Damn it, Holly. Is this what you want? Will you now go back to your drab gowns and meekly hide in the shadows?"

She glanced down at herself, staring at the embroidered flowers on her borrowed gown. "This isn't me, either."

"You look beautiful, you know."

He spoke so gently that despite her apprehension, tingles shot through her.

"Anything you wear will look good on you," he continued, his voice a mix of tenderness and frank assessment. Perhaps this is why she found him so trustworthy. He did not fawn or flatter. Yet, he had a way of making her feel good about herself. "But I understand what you are saying. You are not the giggling debutante. However, neither are you an old dowager. Do you wish to know who I think you are?"

She took a deep breath and nodded. Joshua had a remarkable clarity of thought. She wanted to know his opinion. "Yes."

But she was not yet convinced to sit back down, and he made no move to force her into a chair. They stood face to face. Well, she had to look up to meet his gaze. These Braydens were big men, and Joshua was no exception.

Big and muscled and achingly handsome.

"I see a butterfly yet to spread her fragile wings when I look at you," he said in a soft, deep rumble. "I see the girl I ought to have kissed last night in the garden. My mistake. I should have kissed you and kept kissing you until we were breathless and half undressed."

Her eyes rounded in surprise. "Since when do kisses involve removing clothes?"

"Are you serious?" He groaned. "You don't know anything, do you?"

"I had better go." She reached for the door again. "I didn't come here to be insulted."

He placed his hand over hers. "He never touched you, did he? Not even on your wedding night."

She refused to answer.

It did not seem to matter. His eyes widened again, but he merely shook his head as he released her. "Of course. This is why he married you. This is why he treated you as he did."

He would not stop staring at her, his gaze so intense it bore a hole through her.

Her eyes began to tear. "You are repulsed by me, too. I don't even know why. Will you please tell me what I did wrong?"

"You? Dear heaven. Holly, do you not understand what your husband wanted from you?" He shook his head. "You did nothing wrong. Not then and not now. He was using you to cover up what he was. Not that it's anyone's business what two consenting adults wish to do. But it was not all right that he harmed you in the process."

He raked a hand through his hair. "He liked men."

She nodded. "Yes, he had two very good friends who joined us for supper quite often. They usually stayed until well after I had retired. One of them was a lifelong friend. They were inseparable."

"No, Holly. He *liked* men."

"You just said that. I still don't understand what you mean." Her lips began to quiver. "I'm not trying to be dense. Obviously, I am missing something important. Will you please just come out and say whatever it is you're thinking?"

"Did you never wonder why he would not sleep with you? It was because he slept with his gentlemen friends. He didn't have sexual relations with you because those urges were satisfied by them."

She wanted to slap Joshua. She truly did. But something held her back, perhaps the realization he was speaking the truth.

She had tried to deny it to herself, tried to bury it in the deepest recesses of her heart. She had suspected it, then set her suspicions aside because everyone around her had done such a good job of pretending it was not so, especially his parents who would go to their graves denying his predilections. Walter had done everything possible to hide the truth, and she'd gone right along with it.

She closed her eyes as a shudder ran through her. "I couldn't bring myself to think it, never to believe it."

"To be caught with another man would have meant his ruin," he continued softly. "At the very least, his father would have cut him off without a shilling. It's obvious that bastard is the unforgiving sort."

She nodded. "Indeed, he is. Not even time has mellowed him. In truth, he was always very hard on Walter."

"This is why Walter married you, a naïve, seventeen-year-old girl. A quiet, obedient girl who showed traits of loyalty, duty, and compassion."

"We'd known each other for years. York may be one of England's larger cities, but our social circle was quite small."

"This is how he came to choose you. Quiet and loyal, as I said. More importantly, he knew you had a tendency to keep things to yourself. You did not run to others with your troubles. He trusted you would not complain about him to anyone."

She felt like a nail being pounded into a block of wood, and Joshua was wielding the hammer. Naïve, he'd said with the first pound of his hammer. Quiet. Obedient. Allowed her worries to eat at her gut rather than share them with anyone. *Pound. Pound. Pound.*

Joshua understood her better than she understood herself. So had Walter, obviously. She had been an unwitting part of his masquerade. "You must think I'm an idiot."

"Not at all. You were raised in a genteel household. Only sisters, and younger ones at that. No brothers. Such things were never discussed."

"Nothing concerning intimate relations was ever discussed. Not even a talk before my wedding. My mother was too embarrassed to speak of the wedding night. I had no idea what was supposed to happen, but even I knew his not visiting my bedchamber was wrong. Perhaps I should have spoken of it to my mother. But she hadn't been very helpful before the wedding, and I was afraid she would shrug it off and blame me."

"This is precisely why Walter chose you for his wife. He had it all planned very carefully. His father was his sole means of support. He wasn't going to do anything to ruin the charade. At times, if he feared his father was on the scent, he'd make up some lie about your failures and toss you in the old man's path. Am I right?"

She hesitated a moment but finally nodded. "He was happiest when among his friends, so I often invited them to supper. I just wanted Walter to be happy. He often thanked me, but nothing changed in our marriage. However, he never took his friends up to his bedchamber. If he did, then he was very discreet about it. I never heard anyone but him or his valet in his room."

She sank into her chair. "This is why he joined the army. He wanted to be with his best friend. Stanford was his name. Stanford's father had bought him a commission. It was to make a man of him. He'd told Walter the day he came by wearing his uniform. Walter was crazed when he learned of it. He joined as well."

Holly felt tears form in her eyes again, but she did not want to cry. How many tears had she already spilled over a man who had never loved her? Over a man who was not capable of ever loving her.

She let out her breath in a long exhale. "They marched off in the same regiment and drowned when the ship transporting them to the Continent was attacked and blown apart. They were on their way to battle but died before ever reaching the war front."

"Is this why the Gleasons detest you? They blame you for chasing their precious son into the army."

"Yes, I think so. Although they were never kind to me." Her hands began to tremble. "If Walter and Stanford had to die, I'm glad they were together. We all deserve to be with those we love in our last moments."

Joshua said nothing, merely watched her. She could not read his expression. "I suppose you'd rather not have anything to do with me now. It's all right, Joshua. All I ask is that you keep what I've told you to yourself. But thank you for listening to me...and for sharing a waltz with me. It meant more to me than you can ever know."

"Blessed saints," he said harshly. "Don't go, Holly."

"I must. In truth, I'm completely done in. I'll fall to pieces in another moment. I can't talk about Walter anymore. I feel as though I've been in a nightmare for the past five years. It's best that I just go. Thank you again for everything. I shall not soon forget your kindness."

He surprised her by taking her in his arms. Well, not so much an embrace, as to gently keep her from walking out the door. "I want to see you tomorrow."

"Why?" She stared into the emerald depths of his eyes.

Her cousin Rose, the artist, often thought of people by their colors. Joshua's colors were green and gold. The green of his eyes and the gold of his hair. On impulse, she reached up to touch those soft, thick curls.

The late afternoon sun shone into his office, its rays highlighting the golden hues of his hair. He did not stop her from touching him, nor did he encourage her. It seemed he was just going to let her do whatever it was she wanted to do.

"Why would I not wish to see you tomorrow?"

She shook her head in wonderment. "After what I've just told you?"

"You've told me you were loyal to your husband and tried your best to make him happy."

"I put blinders on because I refused to admit the truth. I played the cooperative dupe."

"How old were you when he died?"

"Nineteen. We were married for about two years at the time. That was three years ago."

She caught the flicker of surprise in his gaze.

"Of course. Five-year nightmare. You're only twenty-two?"

She eyed him curiously. "Did you think I was older?"

"Your sort of beauty is timeless and ageless," he said, groaning lightly.

Despite her turmoil, she laughed. "You did think I was older! How old?"

He cleared his throat. "Twenty-four or twenty-five, but only because someone had mentioned this was your age. In truth, I never gave it a thought. I knew...never mind."

"What did you know?"

"I suppose confession is good for the soul," he muttered, releasing her to run a hand across the nape of his neck. "When we were in Oxford a few months ago, and I'd just met you."

She nodded. "I'm sorry I almost cracked your skull open. I thought you were an intruder trying to break into my uncle's study. I had no idea you were helping Belle and Honey."

"Yes, well. You pack a mighty wallop for a slender, little thing, did you know that?"

"I thought I was protecting my uncle's home."

He rolled his eyes. "When I grabbed you to stop you from hitting me again and had you up against my body, I could tell you were young by the feel of you. I had been told your age, misinformed to be more accurate. But if I had not been told and had to guess, I would have thought you were barely twenty."

"Well done, Captain Brayden. You certainly smooth-talked your way out of that one."

"The point I am making, rather dreadfully it appears, is that I felt something when I held you in my arms."

"Dizzy? Bolts of pain shooting through your temples?" She wasn't certain what he meant by the comment. Perhaps he was trying to flatter her. He'd have to do better. She was quite incompetent at understanding men. This was something she needed to work on.

"That, too," he said with a wince and gingerly touched his head at the spot where she'd injured him. "But mostly I felt...no, I think I'll save my answer for tomorrow's discussion."

She frowned. "You still want to see me? You're certain."

"Of course, I do. Why wouldn't I?"

"The better question is, why would you? I've made every possible mistake there is to make about love, about men, and about myself."

He glanced up at the ceiling and sighed. "You really are dense as a rock, aren't you? Perhaps this will enlighten you."

He circled one arm around her waist and cupped a finger under her chin with the other. "Close your eyes, Holly."

"Why?"

"Blessed saints, you're denser than a rock. Because this," he said and crushed his lips to hers.

CHAPTER SEVEN

KISSING HOLLY WAS among the stupidest ideas he'd ever had. But this wasn't about Holly as much as it was about him. He'd wanted to kiss her ever since they'd first met in Oxford a few months ago.

Seeing her now, looking so beautiful in the gown borrowed from her sister, and yet so completely lost and unsure, had ignited his protective instincts as well as fired his every low brain, possessive urge.

Taste this girl. Mate with her. Protect her.

Of course, the mating part was not going to happen...not today, anyway.

He expected her to push him away.

Instead, she gave a whispered moan and slid her hands up his chest to clasp his shoulders. "Joshua?"

He lost himself in the soft give of her lips.

He hadn't intended for this to happen. Not at this moment. Yet, here he was, swallowing her in his arms, his lips planted on hers, and no intention of coming up for air anytime soon.

He couldn't help himself. The more she spoke of her marriage, the more his heart twisted in knots for this innocent, trusting girl.

He wanted to show her that she was desirable.

He'd never met a more desirable woman in his life.

Yet, she had no idea just how perfect she was, for her spirit had been thoroughly crushed.

A nightmare is what she'd called the last five years of her life. He understood and could never blame her for the damage it had done to her soul. Soldiers in battle suffered similar scars, some of these men, sadly, never able to wake from their bad dream and carry on with productive lives.

He deepened the kiss.

She offered no resistance when he ran his tongue along the seam of her lips and parted them for him to delve in. She tasted of mint, perhaps the mint tea she would have had with her midday meal. He knew it was her favorite.

He also liked that he knew this about her.

He breathed her in, recognizing the honey scent of her skin. It was the fragrance of the perfumed soaps she used. But on her, the scent was natural, subtle, and merely enhanced the sweet scent of her body.

The taste, the touch, the *feel* of her set his blood on fire.

He feared he was lost.

Was there anything he did not find charming about her? Even her prim and proper manner aroused him. There was something devastatingly attractive about the simmering sensuality that lay beneath her buttoned-up exterior.

He wanted to do so much more than kiss and probe her yielding mouth, but forced himself to ease away instead. He needed to douse the heat, not stoke it…not yet. "Holly, are you all right?"

He saw the warring emotions reflected in her eyes.

His gaze settled on her lips, now pink and sultry. Her mouth dipped slightly at the corners, giving her that alluring pout.

She nodded, still holding on to him, and then she cast him an achingly sweet smile. "I think I am very well indeed, Joshua."

But he wasn't. His gaze drifted discreetly down her body, still feeling her against him although they were no longer pasted to each other. He allowed her to ease back, so they were now standing apart.

He studied her, trying to be discreet, despite his rampaging senses.

She had yet to regain her composure. He noticed the light heave of her breasts. She was slender and delicate, but her breasts were full and round and would be heaven to cup in his hands.

He tore his gaze away.

What had he been thinking to kiss her?

This intense feeling for Holly was unexpected. He understood the physical part, for she was beautiful. But he'd read the book she was determined to ignore and understood what was happening to him.

Lord, help him.

He was falling in love with her.

He didn't think too hard about it. Braydens never did. They just knew. *This girl. This is the one I will protect and love for the rest of my days.*

But he dared not mention love to her yet. First, she had to trust herself and stand on her own before jumping into a second marriage.

She stared down at her toes. "What did you think of the kiss, Joshua?"

He tucked a finger under her chin and raised her gaze to his. "I liked it very much. I liked it exceedingly well."

Her eyes were threaded with pain and trepidation. "Then you thought it was a good kiss?"

"Among the hundreds I've given and received? I would say it was the best."

She shook her head and laughed. "You needn't flatter me." Her laughter died as she gazed at him in earnest. "This is important to me. I've never been kissed like this before. I need to hear the truth. How was it for you?"

He caressed her cheek. "Nor will I ever lie to you. It was the best by far. Do you wish to know why?"

She nodded. "Yes, very much."

"Because it was with you."

When she gasped, he worried that he might have said the wrong thing, pushed matters along too fast. She was not on steady footing yet. Comments he would merely accept or even shrug off could send her tumbling to the ground. "There is a connection between us, Holly. Do you not feel it? Let's call it friendship for now."

"Yes, friends." She eyed him warily, but her smile was genuine. "Friends who like to kiss each other."

He did not know whether to laugh or groan. "I won't deny it, but this is not what I want us to become. Friends, yes. Perhaps more as we get to know each other better. That's the part I'd rather explore right now."

"Same for me, Joshua. You make me feel things, wonderful things I never thought were possible. But I don't understand these feelings yet. More important, I don't ever want our meetings to be awkward."

She must have remembered their encounter the other night, for her face suddenly turned to fire. He arched an eyebrow and chuckled softly. "Yes, there was *that* little mix-up. Let's just think of it as a *memorable* experience, shall we?"

She laughed, and for a moment, he caught the sparkle in her eyes. *Blessed saints.* How did any man defend his heart against that?

"No, no. It cannot be called memorable. I am trying to expunge it from my recollection. However, I fear I never shall. You are quite…magnificent to look at. I suppose all the women tell you that."

"I only care to hear it from you. I'm glad you find my looks pleasing."

She turned away and walked over to the window to look out upon the Thames. He gave her a moment before he came to stand beside her. "What are you thinking, Holly?"

"How smoothly these boats sail upon the river. How splendid and right they look, as though they belong on the water. I think this is how marriage should be, two people who belong together. Water is just water without these boats it carries on its current. A boat has no reason to be without the water. They enhance each other, are better because of the purpose they serve together."

She shrugged. "You felt it, too, apparently. We are connected, but I don't understand why. I knew it in my soul the moment we met in Oxford. Does that book explain the reasons why? Should I read it on my own, and only afterward meet to talk about it?"

"I want us to do this together, Holly."

She glanced at him in surprise. "But you've already read the book."

"I have, and I don't mind going over it again with you. I feel it is important that we do. There's a lot to take in all at once, perhaps too much in one reading. Also, what the Gleasons did to you left you damaged. I think you might have difficulty seeing yourself for the woman you truly are. I don't want you to come away with the wrong conclusions about yourself. But I think it is something you will do because your judgment is impacted by your experiences of the past few years."

He did not want her denigrating herself, but he understood how these hidden scars could be insidious, how they could easily slip into her thoughts, and skew the meaning of what was written.

His cousin James, Earl of Exmoor, had suffered similarly upon his return from war. His face was left scarred and his leg badly lamed, but it was the internal scarring that had done the most harm.

They spoke no more when a knock came at his door.

He crossed the office to open it. "Come in, Violet."

She blushed. "I thought I had better chaperone the two of you. Not that I doubted your honor, Joshua."

He laughed. "Of course, you did. I would doubt me as well." Violet had read *The Book of Love*. She knew all about the male, simple brain. His own cousin Romulus had taken one look at her and gone into a low brain frenzy.

He was doing the same over Holly, but he hid his lustful urges better than Romulus ever had.

The difference was in Violet's happy upbringing. She was cheerful, optimistic. Always smiling.

One had to pull smiles from Holly, and they were rarely the sparkling ones that reached into her eyes. But, upon his oath, her eyes appeared to be less clouded now.

This pleased him greatly.

He studied the two cousins. They were of similar size and build, Holly's breasts a little fuller because he couldn't help but notice such things. Violet's hair was dark, and her eyes were a sparkling violet. Holly's hair was vibrant, dark gold, and her eyes were an extraordinary mix of blues and greens, overlaid with that haunting mist of gray.

He dearly wished to see them sparkle.

"Violet, are you free tomorrow afternoon? Joshua thinks we ought to meet again. But how are we to slip away without the family growing suspicious?"

"Oh, dear. Yes, I'm sure I can. We are going shopping because I need suitable travel gowns, that's the excuse we'll give. Not to worry, we'll see you here tomorrow, Joshua. Same time." She turned to Holly. "We had better return home now. Aunt Sophie and Uncle John will worry if we're out after dark. Look at that beautiful sky. Did you notice it?"

Holly nodded. "Yes, it's quite lovely."

Violet hurried out to summon Dahlia and Heather.

Joshua knew he'd only have another minute alone with Holly. "Until tomorrow," he said, taking her hand and giving it a light squeeze.

He was surprised when Holly reached up and gave him a kiss on the cheek. "Thank you, Joshua. Thank you a thousand times over."

She hurried after Violet.

He realized what a huge thing it was for her to kiss him on the cheek. She'd done it the other night as well, that never-to-be-spoken of night.

That little buss on the cheek wasn't merely a casual farewell.

It was a sign that she trusted him.

He hoped never to break her trust.

He was going to marry Holly.

CHAPTER EIGHT

HOLLY WALKED INTO Joshua's office the following day, excited and yet scared. She did not know what to make of these powerful feelings she had for him but was eager to see what could develop. "Shall we start?"

She tossed off her cloak and set it on a peg by the door, then patted her hair and brushed back a few stray wisps the wind had loosened from her pins. The day was cooler than yesterday, so she'd worn one of her sturdier gowns, a forest-green wool. As was typical of all her gowns, there was no lace adornment or silk trim. Just sturdy, serviceable wool.

Joshua's eyes lit up as he watched her enter.

Or had she imagined it?

He rarely showed what he was thinking. Perhaps she was just terrible at reading other people. Well, she knew that was true.

Even Joshua had said the other day, she was dense as a rock.

Indeed, she was.

She took the chair he offered her.

He settled beside her, causing her heart to start fluttering. "We're going to talk about the five senses today," he said, casting her one of his usual, melting smiles.

"I'm ready. Yes, let's start right away. We can't stay out too long. Aunt Sophie wants us back for an early supper."

"Very well, no niceties. Let's get down to business." He had the book with him and immediately opened it to a page that held a bookmark. "This second chapter is on the sense of sight. But the same instruction applies to all the senses. Obviously, you and I can see each other. We have hands with which to touch each other. Noses with which to take in the other's scent, and ears with which to hear each other speak."

She nodded. "And tongues with which to taste."

He cleared his throat. "Right. But what most people don't know how to do is actually *listen* to what these senses are telling them. That inability to properly take in the information they are given is often what leads people to make the wrong decisions."

She clasped her hands on her lap, her thoughts immediately spinning through all the wrong choices she'd made. "And I am a first-rate example of this, aren't I?"

"No, Holly. I was speaking in general. I did not mean to single you out, certainly never meant to insult you. What happened to you isn't quite the same. You had no experience regarding matters of the bedroom, and that is an important difference."

"That still does not excuse my continued ignorance. I could have confided in my mother afterward. Or written to one of my cousins. I chose to keep those blinders on, didn't I?"

Joshua's expression turned thoughtful. "Not quite. Perhaps now, if you repeated the same mistake, I would call it that. But I think of your situation as something else."

"How so?"

"You were staring in fascination at the Thames yesterday. At the water. It made me think of what your marriage did to you." He shifted in his chair so that he fully faced her. She always ached upon seeing him, for he was quite splendid to look at. Now that they sat so close, she caught the sandalwood scent on his skin.

Her heart fluttered again. "Go on, Joshua. What do you mean?"

"You were thrown into water over your head and had not yet

learned to swim. People think that if someone is drowning, they will cry out for help. Often, it is not so. Panic sets in and constricts the throat. Your mind thinks only of keeping your head above water. You thrash and paddle, and then you sink under without ever calling out to anyone."

She put a hand to her throat. "Yes, it felt that way."

"But did you ever consider the others around you? Walter, his family. Your family. Perhaps your friends. They were all swimming around you, so to speak. Did none of them ever notice you sinking and reach out a hand to pull you out from under the water?"

"How can I blame them when they did not know?"

"Walter had to know. His parents probably knew, or at the very least, suspected. Yet they were prepared to let you drown to serve their own purposes."

"Yes, that much is true. But I am not blameless, either. I hid my situation from my friends and family."

"I know your parents love you, but I don't believe they were really *looking* at you. Were you that good at hiding your unhappiness from them? Perhaps not all parents were as good as mine in sensing something was wrong."

He smiled at her, wanting to lighten the conversation because he could see this was distressing her. "When my brothers and I were younger, there were times when we considered doing utterly idiotic things. Our mother, in particular, seemed able to read our minds. If we crept downstairs in the middle of the night, there she was, standing at the foot. If we crawled out of our bedroom windows, there she was again, ready to grab us by the ear and drag us back into the house."

Holly laughed, unable to imagine anyone staying a step ahead of these Brayden men. "I wish I had a tenth of your mother's intuition. What a wonderful woman she must be. I only met her briefly at Lord Milford's party."

"I'll have to remedy that. Now that I'm back from my last assignment, I'll ask her to invite you and your sisters to supper. Sophie and John, as well." He groaned lightly. "Hortensia, too. No way around that, is there?"

"No, but she isn't really as bad as she lets on."

"Well, I suppose my mother can handle her. She managed to keep four growing boys in line. We love her, and at the same time, fear her more than we ever did Napoleon and his armies."

"I don't think you are afraid of anything, Joshua. You are the bravest, smartest, handsomest…oh, well, it seems I've just told you what I think of when I look at you. I don't believe I am off the mark. I may as well add chivalrous and valiant to the description."

"That is good to know. But do you see any flaws? That is what matters most, the ability to see someone in all their imperfections and still love them."

"I know you must have them," she said, a little dismayed. He was right. Everyone had faults. "But I honestly haven't found one in you yet. However, I will keep looking. Is it also possible you are showing only the best side of yourself to me?"

He arched an eyebrow. "There is a little of that. I do behave around you. But it is also important for me to *want* to behave around you. I don't view it as a chore. I like the way I am when I'm around you. There's something about you that softens my rougher edges. I hadn't thought of this before."

"I'm afraid to ask what you see when you look at me. I have no edges, soft or rough. I'm just a mass of unsculpted clay. Or perhaps I'm just a jellyfish floating on the tide, pushed one way or the other, with no direction of my own."

"There you go, being hard on yourself again."

She gripped the edges of her chair. "Joshua, what do you see when you look at me. Be truthful, even if it is hard for me to take. I won't learn anything if I'm coddled."

"I think I mentioned it once before. I see you as a lovely butterfly who is still afraid to spread her wings and fly. Delicate wings that others tried to tear off. So now, you just sit on a safe branch and watch as the other butterflies flit across the meadow, their minds free of care as they fly from flower to flower."

She loved the way he spoke of her, the lack of condescension in his description of her. Perhaps thinking of her as a butterfly was taking matters a bit too far, but she needed to hear someone describe her in a nice way.

His earlier comments about what she'd been going through with Walter and his family were also heartening. Slowly sinking underwater, that's exactly what she had been doing and never realized it.

She smiled at him. "So, I am a drowning butterfly to you."

He gave her cheek a light caress. "Well, you asked me."

"It amazes me how clearly you see me, and how kind you are in describing my faults."

"They aren't faults so much as…circumstances. This one thing happened, and it led to that happening, then this other thing happening. Your nature is such that you keep things inside of you and never lash out. That nature is probably the closest thing you have to a fault. You are too willing to destroy yourself rather than upset others."

"I will work on this," she said with a nod. "But it is so ingrained in me. I may not realize it is happening again until more damage has been done. However, I truly think my response will be different once I take notice. No more of the meek Holly. I'm not afraid to defend myself."

"I know. I saw the evidence of your fighting spirit in Oxford. A little too fearless when it comes to protecting those you love. But it's a good quality in a mother, that fierceness when defending her offspring from all predators." He rose and strode to the cloak she'd placed on the peg by the door. "Come, we're going to take a walk."

She shrugged and came to his side, liking the graze of his fingers against her neck as he wrapped the cloak around her shoulders.

"Where are we going?"

"Just outside the building. A stroll along the Thames. If we stay tucked away in here much longer, I'm going to do something stupid."

She placed a hand lightly on his arm. "Such as what? I hardly think you are capable of making any mistakes. You're one of the smartest men I know."

He laughed. "When it comes to you, I am a raving idiot."

"I have no idea what that means." She shook her head, wishing she understood more about men. "And how can you be an idiot when your insights are so profound and brilliant? You have no idea how greatly our talks have helped me. I'm so glad you were the one to read that book on love, for I would have gotten very little out of it with my mind as cluttered and skewed as it was. If I find happiness, it is all because of you."

His expression turned serious suddenly. "Holly, is there a role for me in your future happiness?"

"A role? Good heavens, Joshua. Now, who is dense as a rock? You are and will always be the greatest part of my happiness. Is it not obvious?" She laughed as she glanced down at herself, at her drab gown and walking boots. "Well, my gowns still need improvement. But you have set this butterfly free. More precisely, so long as I am with you, I need never fear being trapped again."

She shook her head. "Perhaps this does not make perfect sense. But knowing there is someone wise and brave to catch me if I should fall as I flit across that meadow, actually allows me to soar. Doesn't it?"

He nodded. "I'm glad if I've been able to accomplish it."

"So am I." She wanted to toss her arms around his neck and kiss him until their lips were numb. He'd done so much for her in the short time they'd known each other. He saw things so clearly and had the most wonderful way of conveying his thoughts and opinions. No wonder the army appointed him as their liaison officer.

He had a thoughtful and inspirational way with words.

He was incredibly handsome, also.

Good looks, kindness, and intelligence. Did he realize how devastating he was to women? "Yes, there is a role for you if you wish it. But you are the one who may prefer another butterfly. There are hundreds out there, ones with wealthy, titled fathers. There is nothing and no one who could hold you back if you decided to marry one of those butterflies."

He ran a hand across his nape. "There is no other for me, Holly."

What was he suggesting? That she was the one he wanted? "Joshua, think hard upon what you tell me. I am the one who gains by an association with you." She could not bring herself to mention the word *marriage*. "What do you possibly gain from me?"

"It isn't a question of material gain. I am already connected to nobility through my family. As for wealth, the Braydens do not lack for it, and I have a tidy share of my own. What I lack is the happiness only a wife...the right woman to take as my wife...can bring."

Heat rose into her cheeks. "Is it possible? Are you seriously contemplating marrying me? Joshua, is this the stupid and foolish thing you were worried about doing? Is this why we had to leave here and take our walk?"

"No, proposing to you is not the stupid thing I was contemplating. But with this door closed and no chaperone to interrupt us, I was thinking beyond merely kissing you. I wanted to kiss you and undress you. Touch and taste you."

"Oh." That sounded rather exciting and nice.

"The reason I bundled you up in your cloak and asked you to walk with me is that I needed us out in the open before my low brain urges took over. Damn it, Holly. Everything about you draws me to you."

"Oh, Joshua. You're drawn to me for all the wrong reasons. Don't you see? I'm this helpless, damaged butterfly, and your protective instincts cannot be contained."

He leaned forward and kissed her lightly on the lips, then drew back with a sigh. "I promised myself I wouldn't do this. Let's go. It isn't my protective urges I'm worried about."

He led her out, but they stopped by Ronan's office to let Holly's sisters and Violet know they were going for a walk. "We'll go with you," Violet said.

Ronan rose. "Me, too."

Robbie strode in just then. "What did I miss?"

"We're all going for a walk," Heather said, to which Robbie responded that he'd join them.

"Great," Joshua muttered.

Even though they were all now walking by the Thames, the others left them alone to talk. Holly listened in fascination as he continued to instruct her about the five senses, describing the power of each, especially when coupled with an awareness of the one person who could be their potential mate.

She ran through all these sensations in her mind, trying to absorb all he was saying. She loved his touch, so strong and reassuring. She loved the resonant timbre of his voice and his laughter. When he'd kissed her, the taste of his mouth on hers was heavenly. So was his scent, masculine and divine.

But she was overwhelmed by the beautiful sight of him, no doubt because she'd seen all of him the other night. Her heart still thrummed wildly at the mere thought of his naked splendor.

They had strolled eastward and now turned back toward Parliament. The others also turned back and were walking ahead of them, but Joshua purposely slowed his stride so that the two of them would continue to lag behind. "The next chapters in this book speak of connections that bind us, and our expectations when choosing our mate and building a life with this special person."

"Oh, Joshua. I won't be able to visit you tomorrow. Aunt Sophie is hosting tea, and we must be there. Would you be willing to stop by in the evening? Perhaps we could sit in a quiet corner."

He laughed. "There is no such thing as a quiet corner in the Farthingale household."

She nibbled her lip. "I suppose you're right. I could sneak out again in the middle of the night. But that is dangerous. If I'm caught, there would be repercussions."

"Such as my having to marry you? We can finish this next Saturday or Sunday. I'm not on duty then. My days are free. I'll take you for a walk in the park. With a proper chaperone, of course. There's also the invitation to my mother's house."

"Ah, for supper."

"Yes, perhaps we'll have a moment to speak quietly then."

"Do you think it is possible? If I'm to understand you correctly, very little gets past the sharp-eyed Lady Miranda."

He sighed. "That's true. We'll figure it out. In the meantime, would you mind if I gave you an assignment?"

"Not at all. What do you have in mind?"

"I'd like you to make a list of all the ways you feel we are connected. Just write whatever comes to mind. Make a separate list of your expectations concerning a husband and married life. Include children, if they are important to you."

"They are. I think this was one of my greatest concerns when I realized Walter was never coming to my bed. I was young still and not in any hurry to have children, but as the months went by, it hit me harder. When Walter enlisted and later died, it hit me hardest of all. He was gone. There was nothing left of him."

Joshua listened, but made no comment, allowing her to continue. "I felt saddest for his parents, even though they had never been particularly kind to me or Walter. There would be no grandchildren for them to enjoy and watch grow."

She shrugged and took a deep breath. "Then they sent word they wanted me out of the house. I felt only relief at that point, for I realized they were the sort of people who would have taken my child and shut me out."

"You are still young. Plenty of time to have children."

She nodded. "Assuming anyone will have me."

He stopped. By this time, they were about to enter the main Parliament building. "You are in jest, aren't you?"

"Do you mean you, Joshua?"

"Of course."

"That is your protective instincts flaring."

"Nothing of the sort."

"*Everything* of the sort. You've rescued a helpless butterfly. But you must not mistake wanting to protect me with being in love and wanting to marry me. I am not going to let you make that mistake."

"Why don't you let me be the judge of what I need?"

"Need? You are the one who is saving me. What can I possibly offer you?"

"Love. Happiness. Intimacy and friendship. Passion. Companionship. Children. Shall I continue?" He was frowning at her, no doubt irritated that she was questioning his feelings.

"Love?" If only it were true. "Then why, in the hours of conversation we've had in the past few days, have you never once said, '*Holly, I love you*'?"

CHAPTER NINE

JOSHUA HAD NOT seen Holly in two days, and he missed her. They would be dining together tomorrow evening at Lady Miranda's home, but seeing her among a sea of Braydens and Farthingales was almost worse than not seeing her at all.

He'd been angry when they'd parted the other day, not at her, but at himself. She was right. If he truly loved her and wanted to marry her, then why had he never told her? The words were simple. *I love you.*

He'd refrained from uttering them for her sake, or so he'd convinced himself. Was it possible she was right? That his need for her was not love so much as the pull of his protective instincts. She pulled at his lustful urges as well.

That was a polite way of describing the physical ache he was feeling.

She had him in low brain agony.

Even now, to know that she was right next door, that he need only take ten strides out of Romulus's home to be at the Farthingale gate, only made his ache more acute.

Ronan and Robbie had invited him to go out with them this evening, but he'd declined. There would be women and drinking involved wherever they went, and he wanted no part of the womanizing. As for the drinking, he was sitting alone in Romulus's study, the fire lit, a bottle of brandy at his side, and a poured glass of it in his hand.

He had every intention of drinking himself into oblivion.

That is, until someone knocked lightly on the door and then entered even though he'd grumbled, "I am not to be disturbed."

"I won't stay," Holly said, coming to his side.

"Bloody hell." He set down his glass and shot to his feet. "Who let you in here?" Why hadn't the butler announced her? What time was it anyway? Where was his jacket? He wore only his shirt and trousers. His shirt was half unbuttoned, and the sleeves rolled up.

"Violet walked over with me. She's up in her bedchamber, gathering a few items for herself. She didn't need me for that, so I came to see you." She held out what appeared to be a letter. "These are the lists you wanted me to make."

The assignment he'd given her.

He reached out to take it from her, and their fingers grazed. The fire she'd ignited by the mere sound of her voice was now an inferno raging in his blood.

"I miss you, Joshua."

He responded by taking her in his arms and kissing her with abandon, for heat, brandy, and an aching heart were a potent mix. His emotions were raw; he'd missed her so badly and worried that he'd done her more harm than good by failing to admit he loved her. "Holly. *Blessed saints.* You're here."

He kissed her again, long and hard, crushing his lips to hers in the hope his actions would convey what his slurred, drunken words could not. He knew only that somewhere in his rambling, he'd said, "I missed you, too."

He'd also told her she looked beautiful.

Probably told her things he shouldn't have.

So, he stopped talking and continued to kiss her, too lost in the exquisiteness of her body to think of anything but taking her here and now. Even in his brandy-induced fog, he knew this was not possible. But it did not stop him from bringing one hand forward to cup her breast and knead it gently.

He hoped he was gentle with her, but how could he tell in his inebriated state?

Her response sent him over the edge, the sweet way her body arched into his and the tautening bud of her breast as he stroked his thumb over it. "Holly, surely you must know." He kissed the throbbing pulse at the base of her throat. "There's no one else for me."

She kissed him back, the touch of her lips so soft and gentle against his bristled jaw. "I feel the same."

He felt tears when he touched his lips to her cheek, and it sobered him instantly. "Holly, why the tears?"

"I don't know. You overwhelm me. I'm so afraid to allow myself such happiness."

"Don't be."

"I'm sorry if I upset you the other day."

He hugged her to him. "I was the one at fault. You were right, and it made me think about what I was doing."

He felt her hands tremble as they rested upon his shoulders. "I do want to protect you, Holly. It is in my nature, and I cannot change this. But if that were all I was feeling, then I wouldn't have this emptiness in my heart. Two days without you, and I am in agony."

He released her and ran a hand through his rumpled hair. "Gad, look at me. I'm a mess."

"You look wonderful."

He chuckled. "I don't think you can be objective about this."

"You're right. I cannot." She placed her hand upon his chest, and only then did he realize he'd forgotten to button his shirt. He'd felt her cheek against his skin and the soft wool of her gown as he'd lifted her up against him.

Her touch shot a sweet burn through him, just as it had the other night. He would simply refer to it as the night of *the tub incident.*

He wanted to say more, but he heard the click of Violet's heels on the hall floor and knew she'd be here in another moment.

Holly stepped away from him and headed to the door. "Good night, Joshua."

He smiled at her. "Sweet dreams, love."

She blushed. She coughed. She smiled back at him with a sparkle that reached into her eyes.

Once they were gone, he took Holly's list and went upstairs to his bedchamber. He stripped out of his clothes, washed up, and settled in bed to read what she had written. *The Book of Love* sat on his night table, but he did not intend to read it again tonight unless Holly had written something perplexing that he needed to look up.

"Connections and expectations," he muttered, unfolding the paper. He smiled at the neatly organized lists and her perfect penmanship. This was the prim, buttoned-up part of Holly that he still found alluring.

"How are Joshua and I connected?" she'd written. First on her list was the obvious marital connection. His cousin Romulus had married her cousin Violet. His brother Finn had married her cousin Belle. Their second connection was they both came from big, meddlesome families who did not follow society custom when it came to marriage. Farthingales and Braydens married for love.

The rest of the list held more personal connections, although their descriptions were still fairly general and surprisingly sparse. He knew the reason. They had yet to experience intimacy. His body immediately responded in a low brain way, but he tamped down that urge and continued to read. They enjoyed talking to each other. They enjoyed being in each other's company. They liked the look of each other. They enjoyed dancing together. They both enjoyed reading.

It was what she'd left out that made him realize how little they truly knew about each other. She hadn't mentioned that they both wanted children. Or that a happy home life was important to each of them. She hadn't discussed social views or finances, not that he would ever want her worrying about financial matters. One had only to look at her clothes, as elegant and of good quality as they were, to know she was thrifty by nature and would have to be coaxed into spending so much as a shilling.

Did they enjoy the same foods? Did they like to ride? Did they prefer summer to winter? Not that these were so important to know in the first instance, but it also made obvious how much more they had left to learn.

And yet, they were the balm for each other's souls.

Would Holly have confided the secrets of her marriage to anyone else? He did not think so. That should have been on her list, that they trusted each other. Perhaps she wasn't certain how he felt.

He moved on to her list of expectations in a husband and their marriage. At the top of her list was to sleep in the same bed. *Blessed saints.* An enthusiastic yes to that requirement. Second, was kiss each other every day. No objection to that either. Want children. Love our children. Listen to each other. Yes, listening was important. Marriage had to be a partnership where each showed consideration for the wants and needs of the other.

Be faithful.

No problem complying with that. Braydens married for love. They did not stray.

Drinking and gambling in moderation.

No problem there either.

Kindness.

Laughter.

He wasn't an ogre, but neither was he a bleeding heart. However, when it came to Holly, how could he be anything but caring? As for laughter, there would be lots of it as they built a life together. She was the one who held back, who smiled little and rarely behaved like a silly, young thing.

This would change over time, once she had regained her footing.

There was another page to the letter, this one having a list for him to complete. On it were a dozen questions. Some were easy, such as what is your favorite food? Do you like to travel and if so, where would you most like to visit?

Others were harder. How would you describe yourself? What is your idea of the perfect wife? What is the one thing you could never forgive?

Perhaps that last question wasn't so hard. He could never forgive an unfaithful wife. This is why he trusted Holly. He understood her nature. She'd sooner walk through fire than betray her marriage vows.

The same applied to him. He could never hurt Holly that way.

He set the list aside, these thoughts giving him a headache. Perhaps it was best not to think too hard about these matters. Yes, some things were important to know. But marriage was also a journey of discovery. A leap of faith.

How dull it would be if there were no surprises.

But there was one thing he needed to do as soon as possible, a thing he'd put off until this moment, feeling no urgency until now.

He rolled out of bed and penned a quick note to Holly. He would drop it off personally tomorrow morning.

What would she think?

HOLLY HADN'T EXPECTED to see Joshua until this evening, certainly never expected him to come around before he headed off to his post. She had just come down to breakfast when she saw him enter and heard him ask Pruitt to send word to her. "I'm right here, Captain Brayden. Is there something you need?"

His look suggested he needed a kiss from her, but that was not going to happen in front of the family butler. Besides, anyone in the family could walk into the entry hall at any moment and see them.

"Yes, Miss Farthingale. I'd like a word with you."

"Come into the drawing room. We can talk there."

Pruitt's expression was implacable, but she knew he did not approve.

She cleared her throat. "We'll leave the door open, of course."

Joshua smiled at her. "Of course. This won't take long. I merely wished to hand you this note. You can give me your answer tonight." He glanced toward the door, saw no one in their line of sight, which meant no one could see them either.

He drew her into his arms and kissed her with sweet intensity on the mouth. "Think about it. Give me your answer tonight."

He released her and strode out.

In less than a minute, her sisters and Violet rushed in and surrounded her. "What did he say?" Violet asked, giving a little squeal.

She stared at the note. "He said to think about it and give him an answer tonight."

Heather and Dahlia erupted in squeals. "A marriage proposal! It has to be," Dahlia said with an emphatic nod.

Heather stared at the paper clasped in her hand. "Open it, and let's be sure. Shouldn't he just ask you straight out? Will you marry me? Why hand it to you in a letter and run off?"

Dahlia rolled her eyes. "Heather, where's your sense of romance?"

"I am as romantic as the next young woman, which is all to the point. There is nothing romantic about dropping off a note and running away."

In this, Holly had to agree with her youngest sister. "I'll open it now." She stepped away to read it without the three others hovering over her. "Oh…"

Violet looked ready to burst. "What?"

"He wants to know if I would help him shop for a house in London."

Their squeals and screams brought Sophie and Hortensia running in. Sophie placed a hand over her heart. "Girls, you scared the wits out of me. What is going on?"

They all turned in expectation to Holly since this was her news to tell.

It was impossible to keep secrets in the family. In any event, the secret was already out because her sisters and Violet knew. Within the hour, all of her cousins would know. Belle and Honey. Poppy. All of Sophie's daughters, except Laurel, since she was in Scotland at the moment with her husband, Graelem. The news would reach her in a day.

No doubt someone in the family would send off a note tied to a falcon's talons. Did they not do this as a means to communicate in medieval times?

"Captain Brayden has asked for my help in finding a house in London for himself."

Sophie broke into a broad smile. "Your help? He wishes to purchase a house?"

She nodded. "Yes, for him."

Her aunt gave her a heartfelt hug. "And for you as well. He simply needs to find the courage to ask you to share it as his wife. But this is a good first step."

Hortensia sniffed. "Men are all cowards when it comes to marriage." She frowned at Violet, who was smiling too hard to care. "Do you think Romulus would have offered for you if he hadn't been caught doing who knows what to you in his kitchen?"

"He was applying vinegar to my bee stings. And yes, he would have offered for me, perhaps not at that moment. But it would not have taken him long afterward. Joshua is not a coward either. He is merely taking slower steps toward his ultimate goal."

Hortensia was unmoved. "Holly, do not get your hopes up. If he wanted to marry you, there is nothing to stop him from asking you straight out."

Sophie gasped. "Hortensia! Shame on you. Why must you always be such a pessimist? Joshua Brayden is not the sort to trifle with a girl's heart. One has only to see how his eyes light up whenever Holly is in the room to know he cares for her."

"What should I tell him, Aunt Sophie?"

Her aunt laughed and shook her head. "Oh, do not go by what I tell you. The choice is yours. Do you want to shop for a house with him?"

She nodded. "I do. But it isn't proper for us to go around alone. Violet will be leaving for Plymouth the day after tomorrow. My sisters are too young to act as chaperones. And your daughters are all too busy with their own responsibilities. I'm not certain this is proper even with a chaperone."

Sophie patted her arm. "I'll escort the two of you. Mrs. Mayhew doesn't need me to supervise our family meals. I've already given her the menus for the week. And the family will survive without me at home for the next few afternoons."

Holly threw her arms around her aunt. "Thank you."

Hortensia sniffed. "This is a mistake, Sophie. You shouldn't encourage this behavior."

Instead of taking offense, Sophie laughed heartily. "This is quite tame compared to what my daughters did during their debut seasons. I'm shocked they didn't put poor John in his grave with their antics. They certainly added to my gray hairs."

"It's all settled." Violet tipped her chin up in the air. "If Aunt Sophie is unavailable on a particular afternoon, then I'm sure Tynan's wife, Abigail, will be happy to help out. She and Tynan would do anything for his brothers. Besides, it will add to Holly's stature to be seen around town with the Earl of Westcliff's wife."

Hortensia sniffed and walked out.

Sophie bussed Holly's cheek and hurried out as well.

Holly returned to her room to consider her response and drop it off next door so he would find it waiting for him when he returned after work. She wanted to join him, of course. But she hated to admit Hortensia had a point. The offer was merely to help him find a house. And what would society think if she went about town with him, shopping for his new residence, and then he never offered for her hand in marriage?

No, this was not Joshua's way.

He was only being methodical and taking things one small step at a time in order not to rush her. His kisses last night and this morning had meant something.

He was giving his heart to her.

Wasn't he?

CHAPTER TEN

"A NOTHER OF MY boys is leaving me," Lady Miranda intoned that evening, staring straight at Joshua as they all sat around the dinner table. The table was elegantly set, silver salvers and candelabra gleaming atop it, soft candlelight to cast a warm glow about the room, and gamefowl and jellied meats in plentiful display.

Joshua shifted uncomfortably in his chair. *Oh, Lord.* Miranda was in high dudgeon again.

Ah, here it comes.

And there she was, on her feet with a glass of wine in her hand, the crystal catching the firelight as she prepared to make a toast. Others might believe she meant to wish him well in finding a new house, but he knew better. She was ready to blast him to Perdition. "My good son has announced to me that he is searching for a house."

Well, at least he'd been called the *good* son.

"He is abandoning me. I shall now be left with the smart-mouthed wastrel son who is the one I ought to be kicking out of my home."

Joshua rolled his eyes. "I'm not leaving you, as you well know. I'll probably wind up in a house, not five minutes from here."

"Your smart-mouthed wastrel son is not leaving you either," Ronan said dryly. "And why am I a wastrel when I hold the same position as Joshua does, except mine is Royal Navy, which we all know is far more impressive, and we usually ride to our offices together?"

Tynan and Abigail were present and snickering, for they were quite familiar with this usual exchange. Tynan had been on the receiving end of it a time or two. Fortunately, Holly and her family were used to riotous behavior in the Farthingale household. But had they ever experienced anything like Lady Miranda on a righteous tear?

Finally, Tynan shook his head and groaned. "Miranda," he said because she was too tart to be called Mother by any of her boys, "leave Joshua and Ronan alone. We are in company."

She sniffed and tipped her chin in the air. "Sophie and John know me well by now. They are parents and understand how I must feel."

"Lady Miranda, you never need despair of losing them," John said. "They all come back and bring little squealing, crawling objects with them that stick their pudgy fingers wherever they don't belong and spit up on you at the most inconvenient times."

"Indeed," Sophie added. "All five of our daughters are now married and mothers of their own, but our house is still full. We are now enjoying our nieces as they make their debuts." She paused a moment to smile at them, obviously holding all four girls in great affection. "But we know what you mean, for it is nice having a full house. However, John and I also dream of the day we might actually be alone in our home. I'm not sure that will ever happen."

Miranda was not mollified. "Joshua has decided to conduct his house search on his own. I do think he ought to have my assistance. What do men know about such things?"

Holly was seated directly opposite him at the table, looking beautiful as always. She wore a gown of pale blue silk, the color of a robin's egg, that she must have borrowed from one of her sisters. The color suited her, but any color would.

She blushed as Miranda continued to complain. "A man needs a woman's input on this matter. Who better than his own mother?"

He would have liked to cut his mother's griping short, but he did not want to make a thing of it before he'd had the chance to speak to Holly and find out if she was willing to join him in the house hunt.

He'd left work late and come straight here instead of returning to Chipping Way. But he hadn't managed a moment alone with Holly, and then they'd all sat for their feast before he could ask her.

Would she accept to hunt for houses with him?

He tried to catch her eye, but she was too busy picking at her quail to look up. He attempted to switch the topic of conversation, but Miranda was like a dog with a bone and would not let the matter go. "Who better than a mother to know what's good for her own son?"

"Lord, help me." Joshua drained his glass of wine. "Holly has agreed to help me. That is, I hope she is agreeable to it."

Miranda also took a gulp of her wine before setting it down and staring at Holly. "Is this true?"

Holly looked like she wanted to hide under the table.

Joshua needed more wine. Whatever had made him think inviting Holly to a family supper was a good idea? He certainly had not asked her here to witness the henna-haired matriarch of the Brayden family on a rampage. "Miranda, it is a private matter between Holly and me."

But to his surprise, Holly finally looked up and smiled at his mother. "Yes, Lady Miranda. He has asked me. Aunt Sophie has agreed to act as chaperone as we search. I am looking forward to it. Your son is quite wonderful. I enjoy spending time with him."

His mother immediately softened. She reached out to take Holly's hand, for they were seated beside each other. "Then he is in very good hands, my dear. I am amazed he has shown such good judgment."

"He is exceptionally clever," Holly said. "But I think all your sons are. I'm sorry Finn and Belle could not be here tonight. I saw him and Joshua in action at Oxford, and they are quite impressive. Belle is wildly in love with Finn." She glanced down the table at Violet. "And the same can be said for Violet regarding Romulus."

Abigail spoke up. "Me, too. The best day of my life is the day I met Tynan."

Miranda groaned. "Oh, good heavens. Enough of this mawkish

blather. We all know my sons are idiots, except for occasional flashes of good sense they've shown in choosing their wives." She raised her glass again in toast. "Here's to your successful house search, even if my opinion is not valued."

Joshua groaned. "Please, Mother, enough."

Holly was tossing his mother compassionate looks. "He has chosen to search for a home close to yours, and that is such a great compliment, I should think. I'm sure he'll be happy for your opinion once he's narrowed his choices."

"Well said, my dear. But it is your opinion he will treasure most." She patted Holly's hand again. "This is as it should be. Don't mind me. I like to give my sons a hard time. In truth, they are all perfect. But their heads would swell to enormous proportions if they were not deflated every once in a while."

Once the meal was over, and the men had joined the ladies in the drawing room, Joshua sought out Holly. "Is it true? You are agreeable?"

She nodded. "I'm looking forward to it. Hortensia warned me not to make more of it than simply helping out a friend. I expect you mean more, but let's just take it one day at a time and enjoy each other's company. I do enjoy being with you. Very much."

"The feeling is mutual, Holly. I do mean more. I hope you know that."

She nodded.

He wanted to kiss her, but when did he not? "You look beautiful."

She smiled. "Another borrowed gown. This one belongs to Heather. She insisted I wear it instead of the dull mustard gown I had set out on my bed. My sisters are threatening to burn my clothes."

"I'll bring the matches." He cast her a wicked grin. "I certainly don't need you in clothes."

"I..." She gasped and laughed when she caught the import of his words. "This is why your mother gives you a hard time. But I think I like that little bit of naughty in you."

"And I like to see you smiling." Since they were standing off to the side and not being bothered at the moment, he decided to raise the matter of the questions she'd asked of him. "I started to write my answers, then stopped."

"Why?"

"Because I realized that love is not a matter of filling out questions on a piece of paper. Love is something we feel."

"But doesn't the book discuss expectations? Aren't they important?"

"Yes, they are. However, it isn't important to have all the answers right away. You asked, how would I describe myself? I like to think of myself as a good man, but beyond that, I don't know. What matters more is what you think of me."

"I like what I've seen so far...and we are not speaking of *the tub incident*. We are speaking cerebrally."

He laughed when he caught her blushing. "Right."

She sighed. "Do not dare mention it. I shall never live that moment down. In my list, I also asked what your idea is of the perfect wife."

"That one is simple. You. Perfect doesn't mean someone who never makes a mistake. We all make them. Perfect means someone who makes me want to be a better man. Perfect is the two of us making a better whole together than ourselves apart. You are that someone who is perfect for me."

He thought his words would please her, but she was nibbling her lip instead. "Holly, what have I said?"

"Nothing."

"Then why are you fretting?"

She had no chance to respond, for the dinner party was breaking up, and she was to ride home with her aunt and uncle.

He had an uneasy feeling things had not gone as well as he'd hoped. Should he not be taking small steps? Moving forward only one foot at a time? He was ready to propose to her, but was she ready? He dared not rush her into accepting his offer and later have her regret it.

Yes, he wanted to marry her.

But she was a butterfly not yet out of her cocoon. She was still wearing borrowed clothes. She was still letting matters gnaw at her bones instead of coming right out and telling him. How long had they truly known each other? A few days in Oxford and a few days here in London?

It didn't amount to much.

Shouldn't they know each other better than this before taking the leap?

He set the thought aside for now since he'd be seeing Holly tomorrow.

But when he walked over to collect her and her Aunt Sophie the following afternoon, he was surprised to find her in the drawing room with another gentleman. The door was open, and they were seated in separate chairs suitably distant from each other. Still, that did not stop Joshua's heart from shooting into his throat.

The man was about his age, perhaps a few years older. He had dark hair and was rather thin, although dressed quite elegantly. The carriage he'd noticed standing outside had a ducal crest on it. He hadn't paid it particular attention at the time, thinking perhaps the Duchess of Edgeware, Sophie's daughter, had stopped by to pay a call on her mother.

Obviously, the carriage did not belong to Duchess Dillie.

Joshua stood just outside the drawing room, motioning to Pruitt not to announce him just yet. He wasn't trying to eavesdrop so much as collect himself, for he now realized something new about himself. When it came to Holly, he was completely and utterly a possessive arse.

One of the questions she had asked among the list of questions she had posed to him was quite insightful. What is the one thing you could never forgive? For him, the answer was a wife who was unfaithful.

Yet, Holly was doing nothing wrong.

His heart was still in his throat as he walked in.

She smiled as he entered. "Captain Brayden, I'm so glad you're here. May I introduce you to Lord Rawling, Marquess of Elswick? I mentioned to you that my late husband had several good friends, but his dearest was Stanford Rawling. Lord Rawling is his brother."

Hell in a handbasket. "A pleasure to meet you, my lord. My sincere condolences for your loss."

"Thank you, Captain Brayden." He turned to Holly and bowed over her hand. Joshua couldn't help but notice that the man's own hand trembled as he held Holly's. "It was a pleasure to see you, Mrs. Gleason. I hope to have the opportunity to call upon you again."

She nodded. "Of course. Please do not stand on formality."

Joshua said nothing for a long moment as he and Holly stood watching the marquess leave. "Gad, I'm an unmitigated arse," he muttered.

Holly shook her head in obvious confusion. "Why? You were polite to him. Thank you for not giving away that...you knew. Honestly, I think he came here to find out whether I was aware about the relationship between Walter and Stanford. He kept talking around the point, and I kept avoiding it. I'm not sure what he hoped to accomplish other than to renew the pain of their deaths."

"Perhaps he came here just for you."

"Oh, I doubt it." Holly said nothing more, merely nibbled her lip as she began to fret. He recognized this in her, the telltale sign that something was worrying her. Would she confide in him?

"Shall I fetch my aunt? We don't want to make you late for your appointment."

"Yes, my driver should have my carriage out front by now."

She started to leave but then turned back to face him. "I'm not sure why Lord Rawling paid a call on me. I was more surprised than you. He is a good man. His brother always spoke well of him. But the past is not pleasant for me. Indeed, you know how ill it makes me. I hope I do not have to see him again. I'm trying to get away from those years, but his unexpected appearance brought it all back."

"I know."

"I wanted to explain this to you. As you said, I have to learn not to keep things inside of me."

He caressed her cheek. "And I've learned something about myself, too. When it comes to you, I am quite possessive. I did not like that you were entertaining the marquess."

"I wasn't *entertaining* him. But there is a good chance he will come around again." She had a hand lightly over her stomach. "I won't encourage him, but I cannot push him away, either."

"I know," he said again, wishing he could be more of a gentleman about it. But seeing Holly with another man had his stomach roiling, as well.

"You look so dour. I think perhaps it isn't him so much as the fact that you don't completely trust me yet. We haven't spoken of this before, of the basic foundation of a marriage. I, more than anyone, am keenly aware of what lies can do to a marriage."

Joshua thought his mother's behavior had been outrageous last night, but it was nothing to what he was putting Holly through now. All because he was a jealous idiot.

He shook his head and sighed. "Seems I am not so wise after all. I'm sorry, Holly. The thing is, I do trust you."

"Then why are you so glum?"

"I was caught by surprise, that's all." And realized that without a betrothal, he had no claim on Holly. He had wanted to wait a while longer before proposing, but perhaps it was a mistake. "Ah, here's your Aunt Sophie. Shall we embark on our house hunt?"

They didn't have far to go before reaching the first house they were scheduled to see. Holly had been sitting quietly beside her aunt, not participating much in their conversations. But the moment they stepped down from the carriage, and she caught sight of the house, her eyes lit up.

The house was a pale yellow stone trimmed in white. A black iron fence surrounded it. The front garden was nicely landscaped, although most of the flower beds were empty since it was rather late in the season.

Holly liked this home.

The selling agent hurried out to greet them.

"Let's see if the inside is as pretty," Joshua said, escorting the two women into the house.

Joshua ought to have been paying closer attention, but his gaze remained mostly on Holly, curious as to her response as they strolled through each room. She took in every detail and was listening attentively to the agent as he explained the home's best features.

"Plenty of bedchambers, as you can see. A lovely one for the lady of the house, with private dressing quarters. Same for the gentleman of the house, quite large, as you can see. Nursery is on the next floor up. Rooms for a nanny and a governess. Above that are the servants' quarters."

They were shown two more houses that afternoon, but Joshua knew the first one was Holly's favorite. When they returned to Chipping Way, Joshua came in a moment, and Sophie rang for tea.

He took a seat beside Holly. "I think I know your preference. You liked the first one best, didn't you?"

She nodded. "There was so much charm to it. Although it is presently unoccupied, it felt as though it had been a happy home. What did you think of it, Aunt Sophie?"

"I liked it best, as well. It has a good kitchen, large rooms. Good sunlight. It's on a quiet square. I think you shall both be very happy there."

Holly's cheeks turned pink. "Oh, but this is to be Joshua's home.

I—"

Joshua caught her hand. "You must know this is all for you."

Sophie jumped out of her seat. "Excuse me, I'm sure I've forgotten something and must go in search of it right away."

Joshua grinned as she hurried out of the room. "Your aunt is a very smart woman."

"Yes, but she didn't need to leap up like that and dash off."

"She did, Holly. I need to talk to you."

She arched an eyebrow. "Aren't we talking now?"

"I had thought to wait longer before proposing to you, believing we needed to get through that book together. I was so certain we needed time to get to know each other better."

She nodded. "I agree, it is quite sensible."

"Also, I didn't want to push you into marriage before you were ready." He still held her hand and was stroking it gently. "But I love you. I've always loved you. I think I knew it even as you were bringing that candlestick crashing down on my head when we first met in Oxford."

"We both felt it in that instant, didn't we? The moment you touched me, even though it was to stop me from hitting you, I came alive again. I know there is still work to be done, that I haven't put my past aside. It still sends me reeling."

"I know, love. But I want to be the one to catch you in my arms if ever you fall. Marry me, Holly. I was wrong in thinking we should wait."

"Are you sure?"

He nodded. "Not a doubt."

Her eyes began to tear. "You sounded so confident just then."

"Because I am. I've never felt like this before, never felt this *right-ness* with anyone else. I cannot be apart from you. You are in my heart and in my soul. You know I am not the sort to fawn and flatter. This I say as fact. If I lose you, I will lose the greatest part of my heart. Say you will, Holly. If you feel what I feel, then *marry me.*"

She stared down at her toes. "I want to, but…"

"You need have no fear of hurting me or thinking that I will be unhappy in the marriage. I am not afraid to take this leap. Indeed, I am eager for it. The only thing that can hurt me is not to have you as my wife. If you wish me to get down on bended knee, I will."

She laughed and shook her head, finally looking up at him with questioning eyes. "I will not hold it against you if you change your mind tomorrow and realize what a mistake you've made. But for today, if you are that certain…"

"I am, love."

"Then, yes, Joshua. If you'll have me, I will marry you."

He took her in his arms and kissed her thoroughly.

He'd just ended the kiss when Farthingales came pouring into the drawing room, Sophie and Violet first, both of them with the widest grins on their faces. Heather and Dahlia tore in next.

Dahlia cheered. "Now, you *must* have a new wardrobe! No more of those horrid colors."

John was just walking into his home and hurried to the drawing room to see what all the shouting was about. He laughed and shook Joshua's hand. "Whenever you're ready, my brother Rupert and I will meet with you to discuss betrothal terms. I'm getting to be rather expert at this."

"So am I with preparing wedding celebrations," Sophie said. "Do you have a day in mind?"

"Yesterday." Joshua laughed. "I'll leave it up to Holly. But I'm hoping within the month." He turned to Holly. "Assuming you are agreeable."

"What?"

He realized she was no longer paying attention to the commotion around them. Her mind had just drifted back to the past. He saw it in the misty shadows of gray now back in her eyes. Damn it. He had rushed her.

What had he done?

CHAPTER ELEVEN

"HOLLY, IS IT a mistake?" Joshua asked as they rode in his carriage to Lady Miranda's home. It was now early evening, and the air was thick and wet, hanging heavy upon them like a shroud.

She did not immediately respond as they made their way along the streets lit by lamplight.

Joshua had mentioned Ronan, Tynan, and Abigail would be dining with their mother. He hoped to catch them all at once to relay the good news. So why did she feel as though a gloom had descended upon her? It wasn't merely the weather that was oppressive.

She loved him, that was not in doubt.

So why was her stomach in a twist?

Fear of marriage, perhaps.

She sighed and shook her head. "I know you are nothing like Walter. Ours will be a true marriage. I want a life with you, so how can marrying you be a mistake? But I find I am not as free of the past as I wish to be. Those memories have a strong grip on me."

He was sitting beside her and put his arm around her. "They'll fade as we make our own."

She nodded. "I know this in my heart."

"Is something else troubling you? You are nibbling your lip again."

"It is my *tell*, isn't it?" she said, referring to a term used by gamblers to find the weakness in other players. "I suppose it is a good thing. I want you to know when I am worried. Yes, there is something else.

But it's so personal…"

"Holly, you can tell me anything. Especially the things that trouble you deepest. This is what a commitment to each other means."

"Yes, this is how it should be." She let out a breath. "You are the only one who knows this, and so you are the only one I can ask. You see, I've never been with a man. I know nothing of such things and don't know what to do."

He arched an eyebrow. "And you think this displeases me?"

She laughed lightly. "No. I think this pleases you immensely. The thought of someone else tasting my *biscuits* before you did could not have been easy for you to accept. But as you know, I am untouched."

"So, your biscuits are all mine to savor?" He arched a wicked eyebrow. "Why does this worry you?"

"What if you don't like them?"

"You really know nothing of men, do you? There is not a chance. With a face and body like yours? And the sweet scent of you? The sight of you naked? Your hair unbound and spilling over your shoulders. Don't make me think of it, or I'll have the driver take another turn around the square while I prove to you why we shall have no problem in that regard. Do you always worry this much?"

She shrugged. "This is important to me. No one else knows what happened…or rather, did not happen, between Walter and me. To confide in them and seek their advice would reveal the secret I've carried these past five years. So how can I ask anyone? Yet, I want to get it right."

"You will, Holly. I think I had better marry you fast before you have time to worry about what else you're getting into." His expression sobered. "Seriously, I think we ought to marry before the week is out. I don't want you haunted by dreams of the past. Nor do I want to be chasing a runaway bride."

She agreed. "I would never run away from you. You're the one person I would always run toward."

"Remember that, sweetheart. I will always protect you." He emitted a soft groan. "Ah, here we are. Ready to break the news to my mother?"

She nodded.

Lady Miranda took the news exceedingly well. "I cannot imagine anyone more perfect for my son," she said and smothered Holly in a heartfelt embrace.

Holly's head was spinning as the next few days passed in a whirl. She hardly had a moment to breathe, but it was all for a good purpose. She had daily morning visits to the modiste, which she termed "Farthingale festivals" since all her female cousins presently in town managed to show up at the exact hour of her appointment. Madame de Bressard kept her composure as her cousins expressed their opinions on the fabrics, colors, and styles of gowns that suited her best.

Holly chose her favorites, mostly the lighter pastels for silks, and darker blues and greens for her woolen gowns. Most had lace or ribbon trim, but never too much. She still preferred the simpler styles.

Her afternoons were taken up mostly overseeing repairs and decoration of the house Joshua had just purchased for them. Most of the repairs were minor and easily handled. Dahlia had a talent for decorating, so Holly went along with most of her suggestions. Even Lady Miranda was impressed. "Holly, it will be a beautiful home. You and my son are going to be very happy here."

On the day before the wedding, she had Joshua drop her off at the new house early so she could let the workmen in to complete the final touches. Furniture was also due to arrive today. Not all of it by any means, just a few pieces to give them a place to sit and take tea in the parlor. A bed for the chamber she would share with Joshua.

She was walking through the main rooms, inspecting the fresh coats of paint, when someone knocked at the front door. Expecting the workmen, she rushed to let them in. She wasn't expecting the bedraggled man before her. "Lord Rawling, what are you doing here?

What's happened to you?"

A feeling of unease swept over her.

Instead of letting him in, she tried to step outside, for he looked frightful. His complexion was sallow, and his eyes had dark shadows under them, as though he hadn't slept in days. Also, there was a slightly putrid scent about him, as though he hadn't bathed in days. Yet, he did not look dirty.

He made his way past her and closed the door behind them. "Forgive me, Mrs. Gleason. But I need a moment of your time."

"Not here, my lord. You know it isn't proper. Have you been following me?"

She attempted to leave, but he was bigger than she was and easily blocked her path. "Please, I mean you no harm."

"Then leave right away and call upon me when I am with my husband." She wasn't married yet, but she already thought of Joshua as that. "If you have been following me around, you know that I am to be married tomorrow. I shall no longer be Mrs. Gleason, but Mrs. Brayden."

"And I do wish you every happiness." His hands began to tremble. She would have thought him drunk, but he did not reek of spirits. She did not know what to make of his appearance.

Where were those workmen?

"This is why I had to see you today." He took a step toward her, the look in his eyes quite intense.

She darted back; however, she did not want to get too far away from the front door. The moment she had the chance, she was going to run out shrieking. "To what purpose?" She tucked her hands behind her back to hide her own trembling.

Had there been a pipe or block of wood, anything with which to defend herself, she would have grabbed it. But the house was empty, especially the entry hall which had been cleaned out yesterday. There was nothing here. Not even a speck of dust.

He took another step toward her. "I—"

The door suddenly swung open, almost hitting both of them. "Holly, love. I forgot to mention—"

Lord Rawling tore past Joshua and ran down the street.

"What the hell?" Joshua was about to run after him, then noticed she was unsteady. He took her in his arms as she fell against him. "Are you hurt? What was he doing here? What did he want with you?"

"I don't know. I think he's been following me." She struggled to catch her breath. "He came in as soon as you left. The workmen aren't here yet."

"Damn. I shouldn't have left you alone. This is my fault."

"No, it isn't. There should have been a dozen men crawling all over the place by now. I'm so glad you came back, though. He gave me such a bad feeling. What did you forget to mention?"

He shook his head and groaned. "Stupidest reason. Ronan asked if he could borrow *The Book of Love*. I keep forgetting to ask you. It popped into my head just now, and I thought I should tell you before I forgot again. Thank goodness I turned back. Well, I won't catch him now. Do you know where he is staying?"

"No, he never mentioned it. But it can't be too difficult to find out whether his family owns a home in town." She looked up at him, suddenly alarmed. "You mustn't go after him on your own. Let me file a report with the authorities."

"And say what? That he visited you without an invitation? What can they do? He's a marquess. They wouldn't touch him even if he committed murder. I'll find him and have a serious talk with him."

She saw the steel glint in his eyes, and it alarmed her all the more. "And what will they do to you if you hit a marquess? You know it is against the law. You're the one who will end up imprisoned. You're right. Leave it alone, Joshua. You've probably scared him off for good. In any event, how can you protect me if the authorities arrest you?"

"I'll only have a chat with him."

He wasn't fooling her in the least. "Since when do fists talk? We're to be married tomorrow. You must stay close to me until then. Even afterward, don't approach him. Let's call upon Finn's Bow Street runner, Homer Barrow. He'll be more adept at investigating Lord Rawling. And we can ask him to put a man on to guard me for a few days. I doubt the marquess will linger in town much longer than that."

She jumped when there was another knock at the door.

"He frightened the wits out of you, didn't he? You're still shaking like a leaf." Joshua drew her behind him and peered out the window. "The workmen."

Holly put a hand to her pattering heart. "Oh, thank goodness."

He let them in, but then took firm hold of her hand and did not let it go. "I'll wait until someone in the family arrives to stay with you. Then I'll go straight to Mr. Barrow's office. Do you know how to handle a pistol?"

"No." She stopped him when he was about to reach into his boot to give her the one he always kept hidden there. "I'll probably shoot off my own toe."

"Holly, I cannot leave you unprotected."

"The workmen are with me now. And my sisters are sure to come by soon. Violet, too. She's postponed her trip to Plymouth until the day after our wedding. Your mother and Abigail will come by as well. Too bad your mother was not here with me earlier. She would have wrestled the marquess to the ground."

Joshua grinned wryly. "With one arm tied behind her back, too."

He ran a hand through his hair, obviously shaken by what might have happened had he not returned when he did. "Keep the window to the bedchamber you share with Violet securely shut tonight. If you are able to climb up and down those tree branches, so can that devil."

She nodded. "Oh, don't say that. He cannot be that insistent on talking to me."

When his mother and Abigail arrived an hour later, he ordered them to remain with her and not let her out of their sight. He quickly explained what had happened and then left to retain Mr. Barrow's services.

Holly expected he would report to work, as well. Ronan and Robbie were there and would cover for him if he felt the need to rush back to her.

"How awful!" Abigail gave her a hug.

"I shall shoot the bounder between the eyes if he dares show his face here again," Miranda said, withdrawing a pistol from her reticule. "I am not afraid of him. I've handled worse villains."

In truth, Holly was at ease so long as others remained with her. "I wouldn't call him a villain so much as a troubled man. He did not harm me, but I had a very bad feeling about him. Perhaps it was all in my head, and he is completely innocent in his intentions."

Still, she wondered what had been going through Lord Rawling's mind. What could he possibly want with her? To reminisce about his brother? If so, why choose her? Surely, he had close friends of his own he could confide in. She had never traveled in his more elevated social circle in York. They'd only known each other in passing, if that.

His unexpected visit had rattled her, and she would not deny it. But what unsettled her most was her inability to shed the past.

First the Gleasons and now Lord Rawling. Would she ever be able to break away?

The rest of the day passed uneventfully, but it did not calm her down.

Most brides were too excited and happy to sleep the night before their wedding. She was too scared. Her eyes played tricks on her, and every innocent shadow in the room appeared to be a hulking form coming after her.

The shadows of her past giving her nightmares.

By morning, she was exhausted.

Violet took one look at her and sighed. "Joshua hired Bow Street runners to guard the house. He probably stayed up all night with Ronan and Robbie, scouting the nearby streets. The two of you will be the most bedraggled wedding couple ever to stand before the minister."

Holly groaned. "Now that it's daylight and everyone is starting to stir, I'll be able to relax. Joshua and I will sleep tonight."

Violet giggled. "No, you won't. That man will not be keeping his hands off you. But you know how it is on your wedding night."

She nodded. "Oh, yes."

Joshua was the only one who knew she was lying through her teeth. Which was why, much as she had wanted to turn to Violet or any of her other married cousins for advice, she could not do it.

This would be a repeat of her first wedding night.

Well, not quite the same. Joshua was going to make her his wife truly.

She trusted him to understand her ignorance and be patient with her.

The wedding took place in John and Sophie's home, the ceremony occurring first in their garden. The day was sunny and crisp, the sky a glorious blue. Holly could not take her eyes off Joshua as they exchanged their vows, for he looked so handsome in his dress uniform. Medals were pinned to his jacket, stretching across the left side of his broad chest.

Her wedding gown was a lovely tea rose silk.

All the ladies admired it.

"Do you, Hollyhocks Farthingale take…"

Ugh! Her name. She'd forgotten to tell the minister not to call her that. And now Joshua was grinning at her as he squeezed her hand. Of course, his name was perfect. Joshua William Brayden.

Everyone rushed to surround her as soon as the ceremony was over.

She was now Joshua's wife.

She couldn't believe it. If this was a dream, she did not want to be awakened from it. But his touch felt real, and his kisses felt warm and splendid.

Afterward, everyone went indoors to dine.

"Are you hungry, Mrs. Hollyhocks Brayden?" Joshua asked, trying to coax her into a lighter mood.

"Ours will be the shortest marriage in the London records if you call me by that horrid name again. I don't know what my parents were thinking. Holly is a perfectly fine name. But no, my mother loves her hollyhocks, and so this is what they named their firstborn girl."

He still regarded her with concern. He'd noticed she hadn't eaten much during the wedding breakfast.

She shook her head and sighed. "I'm fine, Joshua. And so very happy. I know I've hardly touched my plate, but I'm too excited to eat."

"Or too scared?"

She didn't know whether he was referring to the marquess or talking about their wedding night. "No, I'm never scared when I'm with you."

When darkness fell, as it did early at this time of the year, their guests began to take their leave.

Joshua took her hand in his. "Come, my love. Time to be on our way as well."

"Because we have miles to travel?" She laughed. "We are only walking next door. It was nice of Violet to give us her home since ours isn't ready yet."

"Slight change in plans. We aren't staying next door."

She thought he was jesting at first. "You're serious."

He nodded.

"Where are we going? And why?"

CHAPTER TWELVE

"A SHIP?" HOLLY said as their carriage drew up to a pier, and she saw the elegant vessel anchored there. The sky was clear, and it was a beautiful, moonlit night. She knew the stars would be visible later, once the sun had fully disappeared off the horizon.

The October breeze was stronger off the water, so she drew her cloak more securely about her shoulders. Joshua stepped down from the carriage and placed his hands on her waist to help her down. "It is a yacht to be precise. Belongs to the Earl of Hume. Robbie's cousin is Thaddius MacLauren, who is heir to the Earl of Hume, whose vessel happens to be here at the moment. The earl won't need it for another fortnight at the earliest."

"So, he just offered it to us? But we're strangers to him."

Joshua shrugged. "Not so. We're more like distant family. There's a connection to Robbie, of course. But when Thaddius was courting Penelope Sherbourne, the earl was a guest at Sherbourne Manor and met your cousin Poppy, who is married to Penelope's brother, the Earl of Welles. Robbie only needed to mention it was for Poppy's cousin, and the earl was more than happy to oblige."

Holly laughed. "I still don't see the connection, but who am I to complain? It's a beautiful boat."

"It's all ours for the next few days."

He did not rush her onto it, merely stood by her side as she took it all in. It was as though he already understood her deliberate nature.

She had become like this after her years with Walter, ruing that mistake and determined not to make another. She now needed to know what she was getting into before she took a step forward.

Oddly, with Joshua, she'd known from the moment he'd touched her.

"What do you think, love?"

"Yes, I'm ready." There was something quite calming about the gentle lapping of waves against the hull and the soft groans of the ropes that strained against the yacht's mooring.

He led her up the gangplank and onto the deck where the captain and several crewmen were standing in wait.

A big man with a crown of thick, red hair stepped forward. "Captain Archibald Hume at yer service, Mrs. Brayden. Good to see ye again, Joshua."

"Been a while, Archie." They shook hands and then exchanged hearty claps on the shoulder. "Good to see you, too."

The captain personally led them to the master cabin, no doubt where the earl slept when he was on board. He lit the wall sconces; otherwise, they would be stumbling in the dark. The cabin was surprisingly large, and the mahogany woodwork was beautiful, especially in the warm glow of the lights. The earl's quarters contained a bed large enough to sleep two, a writing desk and two chairs, a chest of drawers built into the wall, and shelves that contained an assortment of books.

The desk also served as a dining table, and on it stood a vase with a dozen red roses, a pot of tea and cups, scones, cheese, and fruit. There was also a bottle of wine and crystal glasses beside the vase of flowers.

"If ye run out of supplies," the captain said with a wink, "just call for us, and we'll bring ye whatever ye need."

Holly turned to Joshua, unable to contain her blush. "All this for us?"

"I thought you might like it, love." He secured the latch once the captain had departed. "There's a basin and ewer in this alcove and more of whatever else we might need in the earl's dressing room." He pointed to what looked to be a cupboard door but led to a connected room filled with neat rows of the earl's clothing, another chair, bureau, mirror, and grooming accessories.

She stepped back into the bedchamber and went to peer out the porthole when she heard crewmen calling out. "Oh, we're pulling away from the pier."

She was excited now that they were about to be under sail. The vessel was sturdy, and Holly felt its gentle rocking as it drew away from land. "Where are we going? Anywhere in particular?"

"Just up to Harwich and then back. We won't sail far tonight, just enough to get us out of London."

She pursed her lips. "What are you not telling me?"

He ran a hand through his hair and sighed. "I did not want to distress you tonight. This is our wedding night, and I don't want you thinking of anything but my glorious body under your complete control."

She walked over to him and nestled against his chest. "But I will imagine the worst unless you tell me. Is it something to do with Lord Rawling?"

He sighed again and nodded, circling his arms around her. "He isn't quite right in the head. Mr. Barrow reported it to me this morning. His father, the Duke of Ismere, is in London and has been searching for him as well. The duke's Bow Street runner knows Mr. Barrow and took him immediately to meet the duke."

"Oh, the poor man must be at the end of his rope if he'd deign to meet with another Bow Street runner."

"The duke is afraid of what his son might do. Seems Lord Rawling fell apart after Stanford died. He blames himself for his brother's death. Probably feels he is to blame for Walter's death, too. This may be why he came to see you."

She nodded. "It makes sense."

"But who knows what is going on now in his twisted mind? He may have come to you to apologize, and then plotted to do something more. That's why I had to change our plans, get you somewhere he could not reach you. Hopefully, while we're away, Mr. Barrow and the duke will have the matter resolved."

Holly sank onto the bed. "What a mess this is. Will I never break away from the past?"

"You will, love." He sat beside her. "I know this is our wedding night, but after what's happened, the last thing I wish to do is force myself on you. I'll hold you in my arms if that is what you prefer."

"And spend another night as I am?" She gave a mirthless laugh. "Two husbands and still a maiden. Do they keep records for this in the London annals? No, Joshua. If this deranged marquess intends more than merely to apologize to me, I will not go to my death never knowing what it means to be a wife. *Your* wife."

"Blessed saints! I'm never going to let that happen. I'll confront him first. He will not get anywhere near you so long as I am alive."

"That's worse! Then I'll have your death on my hands."

"This is no conversation to be having this evening. We're safe. He cannot swim out to us. The currents are too swift. He'd drown before he got anywhere close. Nor can he reach us by boat without being seen. The earl's men are on alert."

This did make her feel better, at least for the next few days. She did not know what would happen after that.

"Holly, love. For now, no one matters but you and me. The incredible thing about this low brain we males have is that it never turns off. However, if anything does not feel right to you, just tell me to stop, and I will."

She cast him a sincerely affectionate smile, appreciating the lengths to which he'd gone to make this night special for her. Nor was she immune to her own lust for him. She wanted to be held in his arms and kissed and touched as only Joshua could touch her and make her heart sing.

He removed his jacket and boots, leaving only his shirt and trousers on. He nudged her to her feet and slowly began to unpin her hair, feathering soft kisses along her neck as he did so.

His lips felt warm and heavenly against her skin.

She shivered as he continued his gentle onslaught, but it wasn't from cold.

He slid his fingers through her hair and watched the unbound mane tumble down her back. "Blessed saints, you look like an angel. Your hair's longer than I realized."

"I haven't cut it in years."

He turned her slightly to unlace the ties of her gown, taking his time kissing her shoulders and the swell of her breasts as he tugged the gown lower, and lower still. She closed her eyes and inhaled lightly as he untied the ribbon of her chemise and slipped his hand beneath it to cup her breast.

At last.

She realized she was now bared from the waist up, but the coolness of the air did nothing to stem her rising heat as his rough hands touched her skin, and his thumb stroked across the bud of her breast, swirling and teasing until it became taut.

When he lowered his mouth to suckle it, she suddenly came alive everywhere. Her body, already fiery, turned molten. Pulses thrummed in places she did not know existed on her body. But Joshua knew. She heard him lightly groan with pleasure, and then he stopped suckling and drew himself up to cup her face in his hands.

"You are glorious, love." His mouth came down on hers in a kiss that was deep and passionately possessive.

She opened her eyes when he stopped kissing her, but he'd only taken a step back to fling off his shirt before he took her into his arms again. He held her close, his arms like two strong bands as they wrapped around her.

There was no longer anything between them, only the heat of his body directly against hers. He felt so exquisitely good.

His body was hard and splendid.

She splayed her hands across his chest, her fingers touching the light dusting of hair. Curious, she ran her thumb across his nipple as he'd just done with hers and then gave it a hesitant lick. He sucked in a breath, and then laughingly groaned.

In the next moment, the last of their clothes were off and pooled on the floor. He lifted her in his arms and carried her in two strides to the bed. "I knew you'd be this sweet and beautiful."

Her hair spilled across the pillows as he set her down in the center of the bed and joined her. He shifted their bodies so that she rested atop him, her breasts pressed to his chest.

She felt the strength of his maleness against her hip, hard and throbbing whenever she moved against it.

A groan tore from this throat. "Stop, love. I'll be done before I have the chance to fill you if you keep rubbing against me like that."

She stopped, eager to follow his instructions, for he was the one with experience in such matters. "I'll try not to move."

He laughed. "You can move, just not...never mind. Do whatever feels right for you."

She kissed his chest, liking the feel of his skin against her lips.

Their hearts beat in unison, fast and pounding.

He took a moment to simply look at her face, to smile as he wound his hands in her hair again and took his time stroking it, running his fingers through it. He seemed enthralled as he watched it slide through his hands like water spilling down a waterfall. Finally, his grin broadened, and he said, "It's time for my little butterfly to shed her cocoon."

"Oh, good gracious. Yes." Perhaps she ought to have been more modest in her desire, but she was hungry for Joshua and eager to experience everything their joining would involve.

He brushed her hair to one side so that it did not catch under her as he positioned her under him. "You're so soft and beautiful," he whispered and then began to slowly kiss his way down her body, taking his time to tease and explore.

The touch of his lips to her skin set off little fires inside of her.

Whatever her thoughts were in that moment no longer mattered. She could not think, only feel. The rough heat of his hands on her body. The weight of him atop her.

The arousing scent of him, male and musk.

She tasted the salt of his skin.

"Joshua," she cried out softly when he cupped her breast and dipped his head to take its bud into his mouth. She arched up when his tongue flicked over it and cried out again in pleasure when he began to tease and suckle it.

"Oh!" His hand now slipped between her thighs to stroke her intimately. She felt herself become slick against his fingers. Was this supposed to happen?

"You are fretting again, love. Am I hurting you?"

"No. I...is this usual?"

He chuckled. "Yes, sweetheart. You'd be too tight otherwise, and I would hurt you when our bodies joined."

He nipped at the lobe of her ear, then kissed her throat. He teased it only a moment before returning his attention to her breast, taking the tip into his mouth again.

She grabbed his head to keep his mouth pressed to her breast.

She raised her hips and strained against his fingers, eager to know more of this new sensation that left her fiery and squirming. She wanted him inside her, wanted him with a raw and savage hunger she did not think any woman of good breeding ought to feel.

But how could she not?

A fiery pressure built within her. She did not know what it was, only that it was intense and exquisite like a volcano about to erupt. It was unlike anything she'd ever felt before.

Then she did erupt, everything bursting all at once in a dazzling starburst of colors. Fiery reds and golds and hot blues. She was consumed, her blood molten as it flowed through her limbs. "Joshua!"

She cried out for him again and again.

"I know, love." He crushed his lips to hers, hot and wild, and exquisitely tender.

He cradled her in his arms as the fiery explosions rocked through her and lovingly caressed her until they finally began to wane. "I love you, Holly."

She opened her eyes to gaze at him in wonder. "I never knew it could be like this."

"Always with you and me, love." His breaths were as ragged as hers, but he had a wicked grin on his face.

She placed her hand against his cheek. "Feeling smug, are we?"

He laughed. "Yes, and every other low brain, frenzied, dominating feeling you can think of. Proud, possessive. Hungry for more of you. Pleasuring you also gave me great pleasure."

She felt the hard length of him and realized he had not yet been satisfied. They hadn't coupled. Had something gone wrong? She began to nibble her lip.

He laughed again and kissed her lightly on the mouth. "Stop fretting. We're only getting started. There is more to come."

"Are you sure?"

"Yes, I wanted to give you a moment to recover before we continued."

She nodded. "I don't need another moment. I'm ready, Joshua."

"Ah, impatient for me to get down to business and claim you for my own?" He drew her back into his embrace. "I'm eager for it as well."

He shifted them so that she was once more on her back. He settled over her, his weight lightly crushing and divine, although most of it was absorbed onto his elbows as they rested on either side of her body.

She must have been a wanton and never known it, for her blood was already turning fiery. He had yet to touch her *in that way* again, and the pressure began to build inside of her.

"Easy, my love." He kissed her, and at the same time, stroked his fingers at the spot between her thighs until she was in exquisite torment and could not wait another moment to take him in.

Then she felt him, his fingers now replaced by the length of him. Fire shot through her as he settled between her legs and entered her. His magnificent body strained like a wild, untamed stallion straining at his tether.

His muscles were taut and rippling with tension as he fought to hold himself back.

But she did not want him tame or cautious. She was not fragile, and he was not going to hurt her. She bucked against him, lifted her hips to take all of him inside her.

When he broke through her maidenhead, she felt a painful pull. But the discomfort lasted only a moment. Then all she felt was pleasure and exhilaration as he thrust inside her, his movements at first slow and steady. But as she became used to him, he began to thrust deeper until he was fully embedded inside her.

They were connected forever, and irrevocably. She had never understood the power of this eternal mating dance until now. Suddenly all the tears she'd shed, all the loneliness and emptiness she'd ever experienced, simply fell away.

Joshua's arms were around her, holding her, his hands caressing her, making her feel as though she was the dearest thing to him. "I love you, Holly."

Sweet mercy!

She loved him so much. "I'm yours forever, my handsome captain."

He moved in and out of her, his thrusts more urgent now, each push deeper and more intense. She felt the newly familiar pressure build inside her, and knew she was about to experience the fiery burst again. Fireworks and starlight.

Would he experience the same?

She felt his raw hunger and the power of him.

As heat and fire surrounded her, she moaned in pleasure. The bursts came one after the other in unrelenting waves. She clutched his shoulders, dug her nails into his back as these sensations, never experienced yet long-buried in her soul, coursed through her body.

In the next moment, she felt him tense and heard his shuddering grunts. He closed his eyes as he released inside her. She stared in fascination, noting the masculine angles of his jaw and cheekbones, enthralled by the enormous power of his body.

She did not think any man could be so exquisitely formed.

Her hands were still on his shoulders when he opened his eyes and smiled at her. Easing her grip, she raised her hand to caress his cheek. "I had no idea. I never thought such happiness was possible. This is a wondrous thing, Joshua."

He kissed her palm. "Yes, love. It is."

"How was it for you? Did you like it?"

"I did. Very much." He kissed her on the forehead and shifted them, so he was no longer atop her. But he did not let go of her and continued to hold her close so that their hot, damp bodies stuck together.

She breathed him in.

He smiled. "What are you doing?"

"Trying to remember every detail of this moment." This was their mating scent, the musky dampness that held in the air. This was the scent their souls would always recognize. *I am his. He is mine. We are now one.* "What did you like best about it, Joshua?"

He kissed her lightly on the mouth. "Do you wish to review every aspect of our mating? Discuss it like a battle plan?"

"No, not if you prefer not to."

"Has it escaped your notice? I am completely in your thrall. You may ask anything of me. If you wish to talk all night, then we shall talk all night."

She laughed. "My poor, captain. I don't wish to torture you. But may we speak of it a little?"

"Of course, love." He began to caress her hair as he spoke. "So, what did I like best about it? Let me see. Well, the best is that it was you in my arms and your body taking me in. You're the most important thing to me. To know that you enjoyed it, enhanced my pleasure."

"I suppose I was quite obvious."

"If you mean clawing at me, clutching me in a death grip, and pinning my face to your exquisitely heaving breasts, then yes. Your breathy moans also gave you away. The entire crew must have heard you."

She gasped and sat up, but he grinned and drew her back into his arms. "Gad, you are too gullible. They didn't hear you, love. I'm only teasing."

"Are you sure? I think there were moments I was howling."

He laughed. "You were perfect. Now it's your turn. What did you like best?"

"That it was you." She rested her arm across his chest and cast him an impish smile. "I've hoped for this moment ever since I caught the resplendent sight of you stepping naked out of the tub. I'm glad you liked me enough to marry me. I was prepared to make an utter wanton of myself, shamelessly lure you into my bed. I wasn't sure how to do it. Fortunately, I did not have to figure it out. You were prepared to make an honest woman of me."

"Hopefully, not too honest. I like the idea of having a wanton as my wife."

Her smile faded as she confided the true reason their coupling had been so special to her. "I thought of these past years and wondered if everything happened the way it did because you were meant to be my one and only. The first and only man ever to touch me. The one I was destined to love. At the moment we coupled, my anger and shame, all the years of guilt and blame, simply melted away."

She kissed his jaw. "You made love to me, and I knew someone in heaven was looking out for me. I am meant to be with you."

He sighed raggedly. "I'm still sorry for all you went through."

"It doesn't matter anymore. Well, other than dealing with a demented marquess."

"He will be dealt with."

She nodded. "Until he's back in his father's care, I'll keep a sturdy candlestick close at hand at all times. I intend to strike first and worry about his intentions afterward."

"My brave Holly. He won't stand a chance against you." He kissed her on the forehead. "I hope it will never come to that."

"I'm sure it never shall." They were out of Lord Rawling's reach for now, and she did not want this moment taken up by thoughts of him. "Are you hungry?"

"For you?" He nipped at her shoulder. "Always."

"I meant food. Those scones look good."

He sat up and lifted her onto his lap.

She gasped. "Joshua, we're naked!"

"I noticed, my love." He dipped his head and drew the bud of her breast into his mouth, flicking his tongue over it.

"Oh, sweet mercy." She closed her eyes and clasped his head to her bosom.

Wordlessly, he shifted her so that she straddled him as he sat on the bed.

"What are we doing?"

"Relax. I promise you'll like it."

She was already stirring, and her body turned to fire when he slipped his hand between her legs. "Those scones, Joshua…heavens, what are you doing?"

"They can wait, love." He positioned himself at her opening and thrust in as soon as he felt her ready. Then he placed his hands on her hips and guided her to move with him. She had no idea this was a possible thing, but it put his mouth at the level of her breasts—which he probably knew—so he had unimpeded access to tease and suckle them while continuing to guide her hips.

Really, this was quite clever.

And quite exciting.

She wondered whether rabbits did it this way, for they bred rapidly. And rapidly is how the heat and fire built within both of them.

"Lord, you're magnificent." He fell back on the mattress, her atop him, with a satisfied groan. A moment later, he lifted her off *him* and drew her down against his heaving chest to embrace her. He buried his hands in her hair. "I love the way it spills over you. Golden and silky. I've never seen anything so splendid."

He kissed her lips and then rose, bringing her up alongside him. "You wanted scones."

She nodded.

"Very well, let's eat." He laughed. "I promise to keep my hands off you for the next half hour."

"I will not hold you to that promise. But I am hungry and would like to taste real food." She glanced around, realizing they had not yet unpacked their bags. "I think I have a robe in there. It should be right on top."

It was a thin, pale blue silk that hugged the curves of her body. It did not hide much, but she put it on anyway. At least she was not sitting without a stitch on. Joshua merely grabbed a towel and wrapped it around his waist.

Her heart was in palpitations.

Goodness, that big, gorgeous body and those hard, rippling muscles were all hers to play with. "I wish we could take a full year and sail around the world like this."

He winked at her. "I'm sure the Earl of Hume would not mind our stealing off with his yacht."

She shook her head and laughed. "I suppose we had better not. The army will probably notice your absence. And it would not do to have an angry Scottish earl chasing after us."

He poured her a cup of tea and placed a scone on a plate for her. "I think if the earl saw you as you are now, your hair unbound and your eyes as blue and shining as the silk of your robe, he'd never be able to hold his anger. Quite the opposite, he would be on bended knee, offering you everything he owned."

She rolled her eyes. "Thank you, my love. I highly doubt it. You are speaking like a besotted husband. Which is as it should be, I think."

When they finished their light repast, Joshua slipped the robe off her and hung it over the back of her chair. He glanced at the bed. "We ought to sleep. It will be dawn before we know it. I thought we could walk around Harwich for a bit, stop at one of the better inns to dine."

"That sounds wonderful." When he settled in the bed beside her, she tucked herself against his body. "Sweet dreams, Joshua. I cannot wait until morning to wake beside you."

He kissed her forehead. "I'll wake you with kisses."

"I'd like that." She closed her eyes.

But sleep eluded her.

Perhaps she was too excited to drift off.

She opened her eyes to peek at him. He opened one eye, catching her dreamily staring at him. "You aren't sleeping," he said, his voice affectionately indulgent.

"I'm still in raptures over you. I can't settle down."

His grin turned boyishly wicked. "Let me see if I can tire you out a bit."

"You needn't. I didn't mean to bother you."

"No bother, I assure you." He propped on his side and watched her while he slid his hand down her body, lightly caressing her shoulder, then downward to cup her breast. He lowered his mouth over it but spent little time teasing it before he shifted down and began to feather kisses lower.

She gasped when he kissed the inside of her thigh.

And was certain, she'd expired when he applied his mouth to her most intimate spot and brought her to pleasure with his tongue. "Sweet mercy! How do you know such things?"

CHAPTER THIRTEEN

Joshua awoke shortly after sunrise, not fully awake but feeling quite spectacular. He started to move, then realized Holly had curled herself around his arm and was clinging to it. He gave her a light kiss on the top of her head. "Lord, you're beautiful."

Her body was pink and warm.

Her golden hair spilled over his arm, and some strands splayed across the pillows. She looked like a sleeping angel...rather, like a beautiful butterfly who had shed her cocoon and was ready to dazzle the world.

He tried to remove his arm from her grasp, but only managed to brush it across the ample mounds of her breasts. Lord, he couldn't get enough of them. Yes, he was pathetically obsessed with their glorious size and shape. Full. Firm. Creamy and pink-tipped.

She was asleep, not even paying him any notice.

He was in a low brain frenzy.

He sank back and sighed, knowing he needed to contain these urges she aroused merely by being herself. When her leg shifted over his, and she began to rub her foot along his calf, he gave up on restraining himself. "Holly, are you awake?"

She snuffled in response, something between a snore and a snort.

Good enough for him. He shifted over her and began to kiss her body until she tugged on his hair and made him look up. Her smile left him breathless.

He grinned back. "Did I wake you, love?"

"Yes, you naughty thing. But I'm up now, so we may as well not let all your hard work go to waste."

He hadn't meant to overdo their lovemaking and leave her sore, but her body was a drug for him, arousing and intoxicating, leaving him mindless. He tried to be gentle, but it was not long before the two of them were groping and groaning, she wrapping her legs around him and holding him to her as they hungrily coupled.

This time was fast and passionate, and as he spilled inside her, he knew he was lost to her completely. Heart, soul, and body.

He was madly and truly in love with his wife.

Not that this depth of feeling surprised him.

He'd fallen in love with her at first sight, no matter that he still saw stars after she'd hit him with that candlestick.

The yacht had anchored for the night just outside of London, perhaps somewhere near Tilbury. They'd only needed to get far enough out of London to be certain the marquess would not catch up to them. Now that the sun was up, the crew had raised the sails, and they were underway once again, sailing on the Thames toward the North Sea.

Since he and Holly were quite awake, they took care of the necessaries, then washed and dressed.

He'd helped her don her gown and had just finished tucking his shirt in his trousers when there was a knock at the door. "Captain Brayden," someone called from the hall.

Joshua crossed the cabin to open the door. One of the crewmen stood before him with a breakfast tray. "Good morning, sir. Morning, Mrs. Brayden."

Joshua noticed the man's besotted gape when Holly turned to him with a smile. "Good morning...er..."

"The name's Rannulf, Mrs. Brayden. Rannulf Hume at yer service." He was a tall, skinny man of about forty years, Joshua would guess, although the sun and salty air had a way of leathering a man's skin so that he might have been younger.

"Good morning, Mr. Hume," she said cheerily. "What have you brought for us?"

"Just a little something to break yer fast." As he stepped in, she began to gather the remains of last night's meal in order to make room for this new tray. It appeared to contain a fresh pot of tea and perhaps eggs and porridge.

"How thoughtful of you." She cast him another smile. "Please convey our gratitude to Captain Hume."

"I will, ma'am." He almost tripped on the lip of the door as he carried the old tray out, for he was still gaping at Holly and not looking where he was going.

Joshua shut the door to close them in again. "You mustn't smile at the crew when we are on deck, or you will have men toppling overboard because they can't take their eyes off you."

She rolled her eyes. "Ha! A bit of an exaggeration, don't you think?"

"Not in the least."

"Is every man aboard a Hume?" She shook her head and laughed softly. "This is the Earl of Hume's yacht. The captain is Archibald Hume. And now we have met Rannulf Hume."

"They're all part of the one clan. It's quite a large and powerful family. I doubt they're closely related, perhaps sharing a grandfather eight times removed. Back then, who knows if any of them actually had family names? They probably just adopted the laird's name. Care to eat? I'm famished."

"Yes, let's. I fear you might waste away to nothing if I delay you any longer," she teased.

He dug in heartily, but Holly ate like a bird. Then again, he and his brothers ate like beasts in the wild, pouncing on any fresh kill. Of course, they did have table manners, so he made certain Holly chose first and ate her fill before he polished off whatever was left.

Afterward, he escorted her on deck. But not before she'd braided her hair and pinned it in an elegant bun at the nape of her neck.

The sky was clear. The early dawn mist had burned away soon after the sun rose on the horizon. However, the wind still whipped across the deck, and it was quite cool. Joshua drew Holly against his chest and wrapped his arms around her so that they stood with her back to his chest as they viewed the towns they were sailing past.

She'd brought her cloak up with her, so he tucked it over her shoulders to provide an added layer of warmth. "I've never sailed before," she said, staring in fascination at the expanse of water that had turned from a murky, brownish-blue to a clear, deep blue the nearer they sailed to the open sea.

"We'll turn north soon. If the wind is in our favor, we ought to reach Harwich by early afternoon. Keep your eyes open. We might spot a whale or two if we're lucky."

"Joshua, do you really think we might?" It was as though she were seeing the world for the very first time, her eyes wide as she took in every detail. More important, her beautiful eyes were no longer shadowed.

They stood in silence for a while, she still in his arms, as the yacht cut across the water like a sleek fish, its motion smooth and calming as it dipped and rose upon the waves.

Joshua listened to the whistle of the wind and the caw of the gulls that seemed to float in place as they hovered over the water hunting for fish. Ropes groaned, sails flapped, and water sloshed against the hull.

He wondered if his life could possibly get better than this moment.

Which started him worrying about what would happen when they returned to London. What if Lord Rawling had not been found?

Holly immediately sensed the change in him.

She turned in his arms and cast him a gently chiding look. "Now who is fretting?"

He kissed her on the nose. "Just thinking."

"Fretting," she insisted. "You're the one who told me it does no good."

"Yes, love. You're right. The moment was so perfect, and this is how I want our life together to be. Always perfect."

"But that is never the path life takes, is it? I'm sure we'll have happy moments and snappish moments, as well. Every married couple must have their ups and downs. Hopefully, we'll have little sadness in it, but if we do, we'll weather that storm together."

He laughed. "Wise words, love. I fear I shall be forever your besotted fool."

"That is your low brain speaking. You are merely fascinated by my breasts and my long, blonde hair. You had your hands all over both often enough last night. I doubt you were listening to a word I said." She grinned. "Just wait until my hair turns white and my breasts sag to my navel. You won't be quite so besotted then."

"I shall be even more in love with you then." He kissed her on the lips. "Which is something you would know if you'd ever bothered to read that book on love you were so determined to hide. Are you cold, Holly? Shall we return below deck? I'm sure we can think of something to pass the time until we reach Harwich."

"Naughty man. I see the gleam in your eyes. I know what you want to do."

He arched an eyebrow. "Well?"

"Yes, of course. Although I feel it is my duty to point out that we have just dressed for the day, and it seems a lot of effort to undress so soon again."

"Duly noted, but it is completely worth the effort." He took her hand and led her back to their cabin.

He helped her to remove her clothing and quickly tossed off his own clothes while she unpinned her hair. He wasted not a moment getting her back in bed and into his arms. He'd never seen a more beautiful woman than Holly. It wasn't just her body, although it was warm and soft.

It was her smile and the light in her eyes.

It was the shape of her lips and the impudent arch of her eyebrows.

It was her breathy moans and the way she held on to him as he brought her to pleasure.

By afternoon, they were dressed again and watching on deck as the yacht neared Harwich. They were still several miles away when Holly suddenly cried out. "Look, Joshua!"

He followed to where she was pointing, and there was a pod of whales gliding just below the surface, spouting water out of their blowholes as they broke the surface and then went under again.

Holly had seen her whales.

Her smile was as bright as a sunbeam. "They're beautiful, aren't they?"

"Yes, love. They are," he said as they swam closer to the yacht. He put an arm around her, for she was leaning against the rail now, and he didn't want her tumbling overboard. Not that she would; he was being overly protective.

"Oh, my. Joshua, look at the size of them! Even the baby is enormous."

They were both in excellent spirits as the yacht moored at Harwich in late afternoon. There were several inns of good quality just up the hill from the immediate dock area and a few quaint shops along the way.

Joshua invited the yacht's captain to dine with them at the Three Cups Inn, and he happily accepted. They would meet him there in an hour. "I'm taking you shopping," he told her. "We need a remembrance of everywhere we stop on our journey."

"May we buy something for Captain Archie and his crew?"

"Yes, love. But not before you purchase something for yourself."

He could see she was about to protest, but the stubborn set to his jaw must have warned her that all arguments would fail. In truth, he wanted to spoil her, for she'd denied herself these small luxuries for so long.

Holly was obviously thrifty by nature; he'd seen it in the care with which she'd supervised the decorations in their new home. She wasn't miserly by any means, but neither was she extravagant. He doubted she'd choose anything expensive for herself.

He would not quibble with her now.

Once they were back in London, he would get her something special.

They stopped at a ladies' shop not far from the inn where they were to dine. A pleasant woman smiled at them from behind the counter as they entered. "We've just got in a shipment of lovely shawls. Let me know if those might interest you. I haven't put them out yet."

"Thank you," Holly said, "but we're just browsing."

At the same time, Joshua said, "Yes, we'd like to see them."

Holly sighed. "Yes, as my husband said. We'd like to see them." She turned to him as the proprietress bustled to the back room. "And what about you? If I must get something new, then you must get something, too."

"We'll see. First you. Perhaps something nice for Sophie if we find it here. Otherwise, we can wait until we're back in London."

"An excellent suggestion. I don't know how I can ever repay Aunt Sophie and Uncle John for their generosity. They are saints to put up with all of us."

Holly's eyes widened in surprise as the woman returned with several shawls of excellent quality and beautiful weave. "Oh, my. They're lovely."

"The finest Scottish wool spun thin and dyed in a variety of colors. The expert weavers follow a precise pattern, much like weaving a tapestry."

"How many do you have in all?" Joshua asked.

"Well, these six and another ten in the back." The woman's eyes widened hopefully. "Would you like to see them as well?"

Joshua nodded. "Yes, all of them."

She scurried into the back room.

Holly laughed softly and pretended to frown at him, but she wasn't really angry. "She will raise her prices," she said in a whisper. "Honestly, you are the worst shopper."

"So what? Can a happy husband not spoil his beautiful wife? I'm not in the habit of purchasing trinkets for women, other than those in my family. And they don't trust any of us to select something they'd like, so they shop for themselves, negotiate the prices, and send us off to pay for them."

She reached up and kissed him on the cheek.

He arched an eyebrow. "What was that for? Not that I mind in the least."

"May a happy wife not kiss her handsome husband?"

He put an arm around her waist. "You may, of course. I shall never deny you. But that kiss was something more."

She nodded. "Just realizing my good fortune. So many men keep mistresses on the side or attempt to seduce women other than their wives with expensive gifts. The Brayden men don't seem to behave this way."

"We aren't saints, love. But whatever happened in the past is over and done. You'll never have cause to worry. Brayden men don't stray. I never will." He glanced at the shawls that were spread across the counter and picked up the most beautiful of them. "This is us, Holly. These intricate threads so tightly woven, you can hardly tell where one ends, and the other begins."

She nodded. "This is why I had to kiss you. This is how you make me feel."

He was about to return her kiss with a lusty one of his own when the proprietress walked back in with her arms laden. She tittered when he reluctantly drew away from Holly. "Newlyweds, are you?"

Holly smiled. "Yes, I suppose it's obvious."

"My dears, you make a lovely couple. May you always look at each other this way. Now, tell me what you think of these. Let me know if any of them strike your fancy."

"No need," Joshua said, knowing Holly would likely give him a swift kick. "We'll take them all. We'll be dining at the Three Cups Inn. Can you have them delivered there for us within the hour? For Captain Joshua Brayden."

"Yes, indeed. Thank you, Captain Brayden. Mrs. Brayden. I'll have my son bring them over as soon as I've wrapped them."

Joshua paid for the shawls, and then they walked next door to what appeared to be a maritime shop.

"Do you think we'll find something here for Captain Archie and his crew?" Holly asked. "Oh, and what shall we get for the Earl of Hume?"

"We'll save that for when we return to London. It'll have to be something far more splendid than what we'll find here."

"I suppose you're right."

They bought an elegant compass for Archie and decided to leave the matter of the yacht's crew for tomorrow. They would have all day to browse the shops in the center of town.

They walked over to the inn and found Archie having an ale by the bar. He was chatting up one of the pretty serving maids but cast them a hearty smile when they walked in. He waved them over. "This fine lass is Merry, and her parents run a tea shop in the center of Harwich," he said with his pronounced Scottish brogue. "That's where she usually works, but she's here at the inn to help out her aunt and uncle who are shorthanded today."

Merry bobbed a curtsy. "I'll show you to your private dining room. It can get a little rowdy here in the evenings. You don't want to be in the public room. May I fetch you something to drink?"

Joshua ordered an ale for himself and tea for Holly.

"What is the name of your family's tea shop?" Holly asked the girl.

"The Frog and Quail." She rolled her eyes. "I have no idea where that name came from. It's silly, I know. But it's the most popular tea shop in Harwich. I'll be working there tomorrow. Do come around. You'll enjoy it."

Holly glanced at him. "May we, Joshua?"

He nodded. "We'll make sure to stop in."

The girl eyed Archie shyly. "And you, Captain Hume? Will you stop by, that is…if you are not too busy?"

The big Scot cast her a beaming smile. "Och, lass. I'll be there as soon as the doors open."

She blushed and hurried away.

They enjoyed a hearty meal, no doubt served generous portions because of Archie's flirtations. The fare was remarkably good, but this was often the way at these portside inns. Sailors and passengers came off their vessels hungry.

Of course, food was not the only thing to occupy a sailor's mind. But Merry was not one of those girls. The other barmaids were bawdier and knew how to handle the men that came for a drink at this establishment. Even Holly noticed and quietly remarked on it when Archie stepped away to refill his drink. "I hope she'll be all right as the night wears on, and the men are in their cups."

Joshua was watching Archie, who seemed quite taken with the girl. "She will be, love."

"How do you know?"

"Because if I know Archie, he'll be back tonight to walk her home." That was the polite way of saying what Archie really hoped to do with this girl. But he was a goodhearted Scot and not one to force himself upon any woman. If she wasn't willing, he'd still see her safely to her door. "If any man gets out of line with her, he'll find himself at the receiving end of a massive fist to the jaw."

He took Holly's hand. "You have that look in your eyes."

She tipped her head to stare at him. "What look?"

"That matchmaking look. It won't happen. We return to London the day after tomorrow, and Archie will never stop here again. He knows that. He won't be making the girl any promises."

Holly sighed. "He looked at her in an affectionate way. Not leering or crude. She liked him, too."

"Doesn't matter. It isn't meant to be." He caressed her cheek. "Don't look so sad, love. They will get over it. A pretty girl like Merry will find herself a good husband in time. As for Archie, I don't know if he will ever marry. If he does, it is not likely to be to a Sassenach."

"I would not have gotten over you."

His reply was cut short when Archie returned with a pitcher of ale for them to share. It mattered little what he was going to say, for Holly had a romantic heart and did not wish to hear him speak logically about the chances of finding love. Being so happy herself, she now wanted everyone to be happy. Life did not usually turn out that way. She had been through enough loneliness and heartbreak to know this.

They'd tarried over their meal, and it was close to nine o'clock by the time they gathered their packages and returned to the yacht. As soon as they were safely on board, Archie strode down the gangplank and headed back up the hill. "Do you think he's going back to Merry?" Holly asked.

"Yes, love. He made his plans with her when he left us to order the pitcher of ale. And before you ask, I have no idea what those plans might be. It is none of our business."

"I know, but I can't help myself. I won't embarrass you by asking him questions tomorrow. However, I will torment you now. I need your help in deciding who will get which shawl. One for your mother, of course. One of the bolder colors for her. And my Aunt Sophie. One of the pretty blue ones to match the color of her eyes. And Violet and my sisters."

She laughed and shook her head. "Violet is sick of anything to do with purple. But she will just have to hate me for giving her the violet shawl. It's so perfect for her. Then there's Honey and Belle. The red for Honey, I think. Maybe the green or gold for Belle. One must be for Tynan's wife, Abigail. She was so helpful. And your cousin James's wife, she's a Sophie, too."

"Oh, hell," he said with an exaggerated groan. "I think I'd rather toss myself overboard and leave my carcass to the mercy of those whales we saw earlier today."

She gave him a playful poke. "So much for being my besotted fool for the rest of our lives. How long did you hold by that declaration? About four hours?"

He took her into his arms. "Not fair. I am and shall always be wildly in love with you. But shawls? Seriously? I think any man would break under that grueling torture."

"Coward." She kissed him on the lips. "I love you, anyway. What would you like to do for the rest of the evening?"

He grinned wickedly. "Need you ask?"

CHAPTER FOURTEEN

HOLLY QUIETLY SLIPPED out of bed the following morning and donned her robe before tiptoeing to the porthole and drawing aside the curtains covering it. "Oh, drat." The morning was damp and gray. A dense mist hovered over the water so that she could hardly make out the buildings she knew stood just beyond the dock.

It was quite early still. She was ever hopeful the sun would come out and burn the mist away. They had only this one day to enjoy Harwich. It would be quite miserable to take in all the sights while running between raindrops.

She turned to the sound of Joshua's sleepy groans. "I didn't mean to wake you," she said, trying not to gawk at his body as he stretched.

"It's early still, love. Why not come back to bed?"

She did not need to be asked twice. "I was curious to see what the weather was like," she explained, nestling in his arms. "It's a grim day, and I was so wishing for sunshine."

"It's barely daybreak, far too soon to know how the day will turn out." He kissed the top of her head when she scooted back under the covers. "I'm sure it will clear. Even if it doesn't, we can always come back here another time. Harwich isn't very far from London."

"That's true. Not far at all. Do you think…" No, she wouldn't mar this day by speaking of Lord Rawling. But he had to be in Joshua's thoughts, as well. Could a determined man reach Harwich in a day? What if he could? Then again, how would he know to look for them here?

There were at least a dozen coves and harbors between here and London where they could have hidden out. It would take him days to stop at each port and inlet along the way. In all likelihood, they would already be on their return trip to London by the time he ever made his way here.

"Holly, love, Archie's crew has not let down their guard for a moment. We are safe. I don't want you to start fretting again."

"I'm trying very hard not to." She threw her arm across his chest and snuggled against him. "Mmm, your body's warm."

"Fiery would be more accurate, but this is what you do to me. One look at you and I ignite. Like lighting a fuse to a keg of gunpowder."

She laughed. "Be careful, or you'll wear *it* out."

He stared down at himself. "No, love. *It* isn't like a pencil that grinds down to a nub with constant use. Last night ought to have proved that to you. How are you feeling this morning?"

"Well loved." She kissed his chest. "I will let you know if ever I've had enough of you."

She dozed off again and awoke about an hour later to Joshua nuzzling her neck. "The sun's out, Holly. Your wish came true."

She smiled at him and scrambled to a sitting position. "Let's not waste another moment. Where shall we go first?"

He sat up as well. "Wherever you'd like."

"I don't know the area. I can tell you every sight to see around York, but I'm hopeless around here."

"I don't know that there are any fine castles to visit. There are several forts. The seaside. Shopping. A market square. We'll sail with the tide tonight. I'm sure we'll find things just by wandering about town in the meanwhile."

They took their time washing and dressing and were ready to start their day when Rannulf knocked on the door. "Good morning, Captain Brayden. Mrs. Brayden." He set their breakfast tray down on the table. "Och, ye'll be having a fine day. Not a cloud to be found in the sky, and m'bones are telling me there'll be not a spot of rain today."

Holly smiled at him. "That's excellent news. We were hoping to spend our time walking in town."

"Well, enjoy yerself."

They ate quickly and headed down the gangplank. They were just starting up the street when they noticed Archie striding toward the yacht. He looked as though he'd been out all night. Holly grabbed Joshua's arm. "Oh, my. Do you think he...?" She sighed. "I know better than to ask him. But can you tell, Joshua?"

"Whether he spent the night in Merry's arms?" He arched an eyebrow. "By the look on his face, I'd say he spent the night with someone. Likely not Merry."

"How can you tell he wasn't with her?"

He shrugged. "I don't know. Something in his expression."

"Such as?" She tugged on his arm. "Please, Joshua. Tell me."

"Bollocks, Holly. Why do you care? I told you that he and Merry are not like us. He may have gone back to the inn to see her. He may even have walked her home. He may visit her at her family's tea shop today. But he spent the night with another woman."

"And this is what I'm curious about. How do you know this? Tell me quickly. He'll see us in another moment."

"Because he isn't smiling the way he was at Merry when we were at supper last night. You were right, he did look upon her with affection. But the look on his face now? I don't think he knows the name of the woman he...there's no polite way to say what he was doing. I don't think he cares that he does not know her name. I doubt he bothered to ask it."

Holly gasped.

"And you'd better hide your expression, love. He's been very good to us. I don't want you making him feel uncomfortable. It isn't our business to approve or disapprove of the way he conducts his personal life."

"You know I am terrible at this. I can't hide any of my feelings." She glanced around and realized they were now in front of the ladies' shop where they had bought the shawls yesterday. "I'm going in here. Come for me once he passes."

She ran inside, barely paying attention to the other two patrons milling about as she tried to sneak peeks out the window without being seen by the captain.

A female patron walked out, leaving only a gentleman who was looking at some scarves the proprietress had brought out. She paid him no attention since she was more interested in trying to make out what Joshua and Archie were saying to each other. Which is why she was caught unprepared when his hand suddenly clamped over her mouth. He grabbed her tightly around the waist with the other, squeezing so hard that she could not catch her breath. "Mrs. Gleason, why are you running from me?"

Lord Rawling!

She tried to scream, but his big hand muffled all sound.

She tried to kick him and managed to land some blows, but it was as though he was beyond feeling any pain. Indeed, he was beyond any feeling.

She was still lashing out and trying to fight him with all her might as he dragged her toward the back room. "Don't fight me. I won't hurt you," he said, but the tone of his voice frightened her. High pitched and frail, he truly sounded deranged.

"Then let me go," she tried to retort, but his hand was still clamped over her mouth, and nothing intelligible came out.

Where was the proprietress? *Oh, no!* What had he done to that sweet woman?

As he dragged her past the counter, she saw the woman sprawled on the floor.

Holly's heart shot into her throat. Had he killed her? Would she be next?

She refused to allow tears to form in her eyes. She wasn't a coward and needed to fight her way out of this scrape. She felt a moment's hope when she heard the woman groan and then saw her try to roll to her feet.

Thank goodness! She was alive, but Lord Rawling must have hit her hard. In the next moment, she collapsed again.

Holly knew it could not be long before Joshua came in. She frantically searched for something to use as a weapon against this demented man. Perhaps there was one in the back room.

He was dragging her in there.

She only needed to slow him down long enough for help to arrive. She'd found nothing useful to turn into a weapon in the shop itself. There were only woolens spread out on large tables. She'd do little damage hitting him with a scarf or pair of mittens.

She was still struggling with Lord Rawling when the bell over the door tinkled, and Joshua strode in. "Holly!"

The villain immediately released her, shoving her against a stack of shelves that he then pushed down atop her. The stack might have crushed her if Joshua hadn't caught it in time and held it up just long enough for her to scramble out of the way.

He then jumped back and let it fall.

She heard a loud crash as it hit the opposite wall and took down some of the plaster.

"Damn it!" The collapsed shelving now blocked the back door so Joshua could not chase after the marquess. He cursed again in frustration, for it was useless to run out the front and try to find him. Also, he'd be abandoning two hurt women, and Holly knew he would never do that.

He cursed again. "Holly, are you all right?"

She was shaking, scared out of her wits, but otherwise unharmed.

"Yes, I'll recover in a moment. But he struck the proprietress. She's the one in need of care. Go for help. I'll tend to her."

She knelt beside the groaning woman who had fallen behind the counter.

Joshua tore out of the shop and shouted to Captain Hume. "Summon the watch, Archie! Rawling was here! There's a woman injured."

Holly feared Joshua would now take off in search of the marquess, but he returned to her side, frowning as he studied her. "Love, you're not all right. Let me hold you."

"Thank goodness," she said with a sob, falling into his arms.

"I know, sweetheart. He frightened you."

She nodded.

"I'd chase after him, but it would be futile now. There are so many little alleyways behind the shop. He could have run anywhere."

He released her after a moment to check on the injured woman. "How are you?" he asked, kneeling beside her and taking a gentle hold of her wrist to feel her pulse.

By this time, the shopkeeper was able to sit up on her own, although she was still too unsteady to stand. When she tried, Joshua gently coaxed her not to get up. "Sit a moment longer, please. What is your name? Is there someone we can fetch for you?"

"I'm Mrs. Mullins. Adela Mullins." Her eyes were still unfocused as she spoke. "I live around the corner. My son will be at home and probably asleep. He works on the night watch for the harbor patrol and only gets home as I leave to open my shop. You mustn't bother him. I'll be all right in a moment. The cur pushed me, and I hit my head against the counter."

Joshua glanced toward the door, obviously impatient for more help to come soon. "I'll run to the inn and see if I can get something cold to press against that lump."

Holly held him back. "Let me. It's only a few steps away. I'll be safe enough."

"Blessed saints! No, love. He may still be close by. I'm not letting you out of my sight for a minute."

"Oh, my dear Mrs. Brayden. Your husband is right. You mustn't go out there on your own." Mrs. Mullins emitted a ragged breath. "I'm so sorry you were caught up in his attempted robbery. Are you all right? Did he hurt you?"

"He did me no harm, Mrs. Mullins. I fought him off." She glanced at the door as Joshua had just done. "Where is the watch? Shouldn't they be here by now?"

"Holly, love. I need you to sit down as well. You're ashen and still trembling." She wanted to protest, but her legs were wobbling, and she knew Joshua was right.

The woman suddenly noticed the fallen shelves in the back room. "Oh, the fiend! Look what he's done!"

Joshua quickly calmed her. "We'll pay for the damage."

"You, Captain Brayden? Why ever would you do such a thing? None of this is your fault."

"That's where you're wrong, Mrs. Mullins. We know this man. He is obsessed with my wife and has been stalking her. We thought we'd left him behind in London, but he somehow managed to catch up to us."

"The beast!"

"I don't believe he was trying to rob you, merely gain information on our whereabouts. He knew we'd come to Harwich by boat. I don't want you to worry about the damage he caused you. I shall make certain you have whatever you need to repair your shop."

The bell tinkled above the door again, signaling the watch had finally arrived. They strode in, two men accompanied by Archie. Holly gave them a description of the marquess and related all that had happened. Mrs. Mullins closed her shop for the hour while her son, who had been awakened by one of the local shopkeepers, arrived with several of his friends to put everything back in order.

The damage was not as bad as first thought. The shelves had not been broken, and only a small patch of the plaster wall needed repairing. None of the merchandise had been ruined or stolen.

To Holly's relief, Mrs. Mullins also seemed to be recovering. Archie had fetched ice from the inn next door and wrapped it in a cloth before applying it to the woman's head. The lump was small, and when she finally attempted to stand, she appeared steady on her feet.

But Joshua held out his arm so that she could hold onto it before she took any steps. "I'll leave an account for you at the Three Cups Inn. Use it as needed or close it out and keep whatever is left of it, as you see fit. It's yours to do with as you wish."

The woman was surprised but obviously grateful. "Thank you, Captain Brayden. Oh, dear! What your poor wife must be going through. I hope you catch that horrid man before he does her any harm."

He nodded. "That is what I hope to do."

Although Joshua responded calmly, Holly knew he was quite over-set. So was she. Lord Rawling had eluded not only his father's Bow Street runners but theirs, as well. She knew how good Mr. Barrow was, and this caused her the most worry.

How had he been able to track them down so fast? More importantly, what was to be done about him? More men from the harbor watch had arrived and were now going to fan out through the town to conduct a search.

Holly did not think they would ever find him.

Once they'd given their statements and made certain Mrs. Mullins was well attended to, she, Joshua, and Archie left the shop. "Blast, we canno' leave yet," Archie said, running his hand through his shock of red hair. "The tide's too low."

"I'm taking Holly back to the yacht anyway. We'll stay on board. Archie, let's get out of here as soon as the tide allows."

Tears formed in Holly's eyes, and she could no longer hold them back. "But what about Merry's tea shop? We said we'd come by. And you, Archie. You promised her you'd stop in."

Joshua eyed her worriedly. "Love, it doesn't matter. She'll hear what happened and understand."

"No." She turned to Archie, tears now streaming down her cheeks. "You have to go."

He and Joshua exchanged looks.

What was wrong with them? Could they not understand? Lord Rawling may have upset their honeymoon trip, but she could not allow him to upset Archie's chance at finding romance. What if Merry was meant to be his true love? "The tide's out. We can't leave Harwich, as you just said. You must go to her."

Archie appeared thoroughly confused. "Aye," he said, obviously humoring her, "I will next time we dock in Harwich."

"But it might be too late by then. What if you never return? What reason would Lord Hume ever have to stop here?"

When she grabbed Archie's lapels and tried to shake him, Joshua swept her up in his arms and carried her back to the yacht. She wrapped her arms around his neck, then buried her head against his shoulder and sobbed.

Archie kept stride with them. "Och, yer poor wife is in shock."

"I know. Bollocks, what a mess." Joshua kissed the top of her head. "I'll get her back to our cabin. Do you have brandy on board?"

"Aye, Joshua. Let me know what else ye need, and I'll send one of my men to fetch whatever we dinna have."

"Thank you. I'm hoping the brandy will be enough." He kissed her again, and she sensed it was as much to calm himself as it was to calm her.

He still held her in his arms as he strode up the gangplank and then across the deck toward the steps leading down to the cabins. "I can walk," she said, not sounding very convincing. "Don't take me down there yet. Please. It feels as though we're descending into a tomb. Let me catch a breath of air on deck first."

He wasn't happy about it, no doubt concerned she would make an easy target if Lord Rawling intended to shoot her. But he could have done so in the woolens shop had he really wanted to. Also, as he'd tried to carry her off, he had assured her that he would not hurt her. Could she believe him?

To such a man, assuring her that he would not hurt her could mean locking her away in some hidden prison for the rest of her life. Hiding her where she'd never be found. Or burying her alive beside Walter's grave.

Her head began to spin, and she took in great gulps of air, suddenly feeling breathless.

"Holly! Holly!" she heard Joshua call out, but she was beyond responding. The world had turned dark around her.

CHAPTER FIFTEEN

WHILE SEVERAL MEMBERS of Archie's crew looked on in alarm, Joshua made his way down to the earl's cabin with Holly still unconscious in his arms. He had never felt so helpless in his life. No amount of battles fought, no matter how many times he'd been injured or faced death, had prepared him for the sight of Holly being dragged off by that demented creature.

He set her gently on the bed and proceeded to remove her shoes and cloak for want of something else to do.

"Is there anything we can do, Captain Brayden?" Rannulf asked, almost in tears himself. Holly had been very kind to him, had been sweet and pleasant to all of the earl's crew, and Joshua knew they'd grown fond of her.

How could anyone resist loving her?

"Yes, Rannulf. I think Mrs. Brayden left a bottle of perfume on the earl's dressing table." He withdrew his handkerchief and handed it to the sailor. "Dab some of it onto this and bring it back to me."

"And me, Captain?" asked another crewman by the name of Donnall.

"She'll want some mint tea once she comes around. I'll give her the brandy first, but this is her favorite tea, and she'll feel better for having something familiar to calm her."

"Aye, I'll let Cook know." He sighed and shook his head as he stared at Holly. "The poor lass. She's safe aboard his lordship's yacht. I hope she knows that."

Joshua nodded. "She does."

But what was he to do once they were back in London? He could not spend the rest of his life manacled to her at every moment. He would have to report back to duty in a couple of days. What then?

Even if he were permitted additional leave, what would it accomplish? Holly would not want him following her into every room, hovering over her at every moment of every day.

But twice now, he'd left her for an instant, and that fiend had appeared.

He took the doused handkerchief from Rannulf and gently rubbed it across Holly's brow. Then he dabbed it at her wrists and neck. "Holly, my love," he said softly when she moaned and fluttered her eyes. "You're safe here. We're on the earl's yacht. I'm right beside you."

She nodded. "He won't let me break away from the past."

"But you shall, love. When you're feeling a little better, we'll set a plan of action."

She nodded again and slowly sat up.

As she was now aware of her surroundings, she glanced over his shoulder to smile at Rannulf and two other crewmen who were peering in. "I am comforted knowing you are all looking out for me."

"Aye, Mrs. Brayden. That ye are."

The crewmen left as Archie came in with a bottle of brandy and poured a little into a glass. "Here ye go, lass. Have a sip."

Her hand still trembled as she took a gulp of the offered drink. "Ugh! How can you men drink this?" But she laughed and took another sip, making the same sour face as she uttered another *ugh*.

Joshua took the glass from her hand and set it on the table. "Cook is boiling some mint tea for you. Is there anything else you'd like, love?"

She shook her head. "No. I'll be fine in a moment. I don't know what came over me."

"Shock," Archie said, still frowning as he regarded her. "But ye've let it all out now, so I hope ye're back to yerself. I know he gave ye a fright, but just remember that he's simply a man. He bleeds like the rest of us. He has strengths and weaknesses, just as we all do."

"For him to have reached us in Harwich," Joshua said, "means he must have been traveling overnight. I doubt he's slept in days. He cannot go on as he has, or his body will give out. The harbor patrol has spread the word to all the local merchants. If he sticks his head out from his hiding hole, someone will notice and summon the watch."

He tried to sound hopeful but doubted he was doing a good job of it. Holly's eyes were once again shadowed. It saddened him to see their beautiful sparkle gone. He wanted to go in search of the bastard himself, but the worst thing he could do was leave Holly's side now.

Archie patted him on the shoulder. "I'll go into town and see what more I can find out. We'll set sail before dusk, Mrs. Brayden. Never ye worry. We'll be on the open water tonight."

Joshua was alone once more with his wife.

He'd left the door open since Donnall would soon return with her tea. Also, he wanted to encourage the sailors to pop their heads in to wish her well. "Do you feel well enough to talk to me, Holly?

She nodded. "Yes. I prefer it. I need to keep my mind occupied, or I shall turn into a watering pot again."

"You are no such thing. You were very brave in that shop, fighting him and all the while looking around for something with which to hit him. I saw how your mind was working in those precious moments. You fought valiantly." He leaned forward and took her hand. "Always be a fighter, love."

She cast him a fragile smile. "Ah, if only I'd had a candlestick."

He chuckled. "You and that candlestick could have taken down an entire Roman legion."

"A bit of an exaggeration, I think."

"No, I am entirely convinced you could do it. And I've also been thinking about making a few changes around our new house. First and foremost is to get us a dog. There are breeds known to be excellent guard dogs. I'd also like you to carry a pistol at all times. They make smaller ones that are popular with ladies. Miranda has several and isn't afraid to use them."

Holly managed a soft laugh. "I've heard the wild stories about her prowess. I wish I were more like her."

He kissed her on the lips. "Heaven forbid. The world does not need another Lady Miranda. Besides, I like you just as you are."

"I've caused you nothing but trouble."

"You've given me joy beyond anything I could ever have imagined. None of this is your fault. We'll get through it together. Where was I? Oh, yes. Dog. Pistol. Miranda, who will burn a path through London, hunting him down. In addition, surveillance. I'm going to keep Mr. Barrow and his men on to protect you whenever I'm not around."

"For how long? What if years go by before Lord Rawling comes out of hiding?"

"Then that is how long those Bow Street runners will be watching you. I'll hire additional footmen on top of the butler, cook, and maids we will keep on staff." He took both her hands in his. "Dog. Pistol. Miranda. Bow Street runners. House full of servants. Me. You will not be alone."

In truth, having a plan of action was calming him down. He knew Lord Rawling was devilishly clever, but how could he get past all these precautions?

"What do you think, love? Anything you'd like to add?"

She nodded. "Two dogs, not one."

"You may have ten if you like. Why two?"

"One to guard me, but I'd like the other to be a good tracker, able to pick up my scent if he does manage to abduct me and hide me in a hole somewhere. If I cannot get out, I'll need you to find me."

Joshua's heart twisted in knots. Blessed saints! He wanted this man dead. Holly locked away? Never able to get out? "So be it. Four dogs. Two of them guard dogs, and two of them trackers."

"My love, I fear we shall need a bigger house to fit us all in."

He nodded. "Very well, a new house it shall be."

"No, I jest." She laughed lightly. "I love the house you purchased for us, and Dahlia did such a beautiful job helping me decorate it. I do not want to sell my dream home."

Donnall brought in a pot of mint tea for Holly. Rannulf and several other crewmen stopped in again to see if she needed anything else. He hadn't seen Archie in a while, but he was likely occupied with the harbor patrol. Right now, those men were the best hope they had of finding Lord Rawling, assuming he was still in Harwich.

A half-hour later, there was a light knock at their open door. Archie stood there with a small tray in his hands. Joshua was sure it was cakes or tarts by the heavenly aroma wafting out from under the cloth draped over the hidden contents.

"Come in, Archie. Any news?" Joshua was eager to hear his report.

"The harbor patrol is still searching for him. They'll come to me straight away if they catch him. But Mrs. Brayden has a visitor. I made a stop in town, as ye suggested." He cast Holly a broad grin. "Merry made these for ye, and she's come to see how ye're doing."

"Truly?" Her eyes widened, and her smile was suddenly beaming. "Do let her in."

Joshua moved the chairs so that they faced out from the table while Archie set down the tray and removed the cloth.

"Oh, Merry! Are these apple tarts? With cinnamon? And apricot tarts, too? Is this one cherry? How beautiful they all look. Please do sit down and join us. You as well, Captain Hume. Please stay. We'll need more tea."

"Och, dinna bother. Yer husband and I will have brandy." He

winked at her. "I think yer husband could do with an entire bottle all to himself."

She nodded. "Our first few days of marriage certainly have not been dull. Merry, may I pour you a tea?"

"Yes, thank you, Mrs. Brayden. We were all so dismayed to hear what happened. I'm sure the villain will be found soon. Poor Mrs. Mullins! I'm glad she'll fully recover. My parents sent over some pies to her, as well." She shook her head. "What an ugly business."

They moved on to speak of more pleasant things until Merry made her apologies. "I must return to the shop now. It'll get busy soon, and my parents will need me to help out."

"Thank you for stopping by," Holly said. "Your visit was the best medicine for me."

Merry blushed. "It was my pleasure, Mrs. Brayden."

Archie took the girl's arm. "I'll escort ye back, lass. I dinna want ye walking alone."

When they were out of earshot, Joshua shook his head and laughed. "I'll be damned. Did you notice the cow-eyed looks they were giving each other?"

Holly was grinning from ear to ear. "I told you they liked each other." She held up her hand to stop him from saying anything more about them. "I understand nothing may ever come of it. But it eases my heart to know at least they gave each other a second look. And I know it has nothing to do with Lord Rawling. But I needed to know that love continues no matter what evil rains down on us."

"Come into my arms, love. I want to hold you." He kissed her when she did so and wrapped his arms around her to hold her tightly to his chest. His heart was pounding a steady beat, but he was quite broken up inside.

"Careful, my handsome captain. I could get used to this."

"I hope so." He kissed her again, the touch of his lips light and gentle against hers, for he worried she was still too fragile in spirit after today's scare.

Anyone would be scared to know such a fiend was after them. If the possible romance between a big, redheaded Scot and a sweet, Harwich tea shop maid helped ease her turmoil, all the better.

As the sun was beginning to set on the horizon and the tide rolled in, they were finally able to sail. Once they were away from land, Joshua escorted her on deck to watch for whales and seals. They saw a pod of whales, perhaps the same ones following their boat when they had first arrived at Harwich.

Holly was as excited as could be. "What splendid creatures they are. Look at that little one keeping close to its mother."

Birds circled above the whales, no doubt expecting to find food as these leviathans churned the sea.

Holly's near abduction this morning seemed like a bad dream, that moment of terror so removed from the natural beauty now surrounding them.

Joshua stayed close to her, his arms around her all the while. They were in paradise again, and both of them felt it, even if only for this brief time.

Holly removed the pins from her hair and allowed her long strands to blow wild and free in the wind. She closed her eyes and tipped her head toward the sun, while her hair tossed and whipped about her body like a magnificent, golden sail.

He hoped she would remember these moments of heaven once they were back in London and grim reality set in. They had a hard task ahead of them.

But for now, they would enjoy the sea and salty air.

As night fell, Archie sailed the yacht into an inlet just south of the Thames and dropped anchor. They were still in the North Sea, far enough away from land as to be unreachable.

Joshua spent a while going over procedures for their docking with Archie. He also wanted to arrange for a carriage to bring them to Lady

Miranda's home first. He'd explain later to Holly. She was eager for them to settle in their new home but would understand it was safer not to do so just yet.

They needed to hire staff and acquire those dogs. Most of their furniture had yet to be purchased, and of those items that had been purchased, only a few pieces had been delivered. The others would take several more days, some even weeks or months, to arrive.

Holly was peering out the porthole when he returned to their cabin. He hoped she was gazing at the stars or looking for whales again. He did not want her staring blankly and dwelling on thoughts as ink-dark as the night.

"Ready for bed, love? Shall I help you unlace your gown?" He'd asked merely as a protective husband, having no intention of behaving like a randy goat. He would do no more than hold her in his arms unless she was the one to initiate something more.

"Yes, this day has drained me. I know the next few days will be tense as well. We can never let down our guard until Lord Rawling is in custody." Her lips were pursed in thought as she turned to him. "I was wondering…"

He approached and began to undo her gown. "Yes, love?"

"His little cat-and-mouse game could go on for months unless we take action."

He did not like the sound of that. "What do you mean?"

"What if we set a trap for him."

His hand froze on her lacings. "And use you as the bait? Out of the question. I will not put you at risk."

"But I'm already at risk, aren't I? He is a wolf on the prowl, and he won't stop hunting me until I am in his jaws again."

Joshua shook his head. "You are asking me to hand you up to him on a silver platter. Forget it. What if he grabs you and still eludes our trap? He's done it already, escaping the best investigators London has to offer."

"It won't be the same. If he has me, I'll be there screaming and clutching onto any object I can find to slow him down. It would take you no time to catch up to us."

"Assuming you are conscious. A man like that..." He ran a hand roughly through his hair. "If what his father told Mr. Barrow is true, then his mind has snapped. And with it, he has grown more cunning and diabolical. When he comes for you, he will be prepared to silence you. After this morning's episode, he knows you will fight him. You were fortunate he was only at the shop to seek information. You probably surprised him by showing up when you did. He wasn't prepared."

"Even so, I need this to end, Joshua. *I* will snap if I must spend the rest of my days frightened of this man. I'm not saying we must do it tomorrow. But I think it is a workable plan. Let's talk it over. Teach me to use a pistol. Or I can ask your mother to teach me." She cast him a wry smile. "I'm sure she won't mind. Indeed, if Miranda is half as wild as you make her out to be, she'll take great pride in it and probably show me a few tricks that she's never told any of her sons about."

He groaned. "Gad, do not listen to anything my mother tells you. She will lead you down the path to ruin."

Holly sighed. "I know you are mad with worry for me. That is all the more reason why I must be as fierce as Miranda about this. I want to become a crack shot. I want those dogs. I want us to set that trap. I want *me* back. I *don't* want to be the sad, easily-pushed-around wife I used to be. The Holly, who was Walter Gleason's widow, is a thing of the past."

Nor did he wish this for her.

Perhaps there was some merit to what she was saying, but the mere thought of throwing her in the path of danger had his guts in a roil. "I'll think about it."

She slipped off her gown and set it neatly aside, then curled up on the bed. She still wore her chemise and stockings, but he could remove those quite quickly if necessary. "Come to bed, Joshua."

He did not need to be asked twice.

He undressed and slid under the covers, intending only to take her in his arms. But all his good intentions were cast to the wind the moment Holly touched him. He made love to her slowly and gently, sensing she needed the touch of his hands and lips and the joining of their bodies.

Her body was warm and sweet as he spilled inside her, and her skin held the scent of lavender. He kissed her throat and shoulder, and further down to her breast, tasting and teasing the creamy mound as she soon followed him in her release.

He watched her.

Nothing was more beautiful than Holly lost in passion, her eyes closed and her lips slightly parted.

And yet, his heart was still in pieces.

He could not lose her.

Did Holly have the right of it? Should they set a trap?

And use her as the bait?

CHAPTER SIXTEEN

JOSHUA AND HOLLY arrived unannounced at Lady Miranda's home in the early evening. Joshua took a moment to see that their bags were brought up to his old room, and then he escorted his wife into the parlor where his mother was entertaining family. His older brothers and their wives were there. Ronan was there, too.

In truth, he was relieved. It was easier to tell them all at once rather than have to repeat the story *ad nauseam*.

Miranda rose to greet them. "My dears, what a lovely surprise. It is so good to see you. Did you have a nice trip?"

Joshua cleared his throat. "For the most part."

"Oh, hell," Finn said, immediately catching on. He left his wife's side to approach them, his brow furrowed. "Have you eaten? Would you like a drink? Tell us what happened."

That Finn took command as host was not surprising. Miranda's elegant townhouse was owned by Finn. Joshua suspected his brother owned half of London by now since he was that brilliant when it came to financial matters. Would he be as good at tactical matters? This was Joshua's area of strength, but his heart and soul were too involved to allow him to look at the problem impartially.

"I'll have a glass of port. Holly, what would you like?" he asked, settling beside her on the settee.

She turned to Finn. "Mint tea, if you have it."

Finn cast her a warm smile. "Miranda's favorite. We have it

stocked here by the barrels."

"We've just finished our supper," Miranda said, "but we'll have something prepared for you if you are hungry."

He and Holly declined. "We ate with Captain Hume before disembarking."

He took hold of Holly's hand as he proceeded to relate all that had happened. He wanted the opinion of his brothers before finalizing any plan that would involve putting Holly at risk.

Money was no object, either. All the Braydens had wealth of their own. None of the Brayden men were spendthrifts or reprobates; it simply wasn't in their blood. But they'd achieved their wealth mostly because of Finn's brilliance. He had a knack for investing, for taking a shilling and somehow turning it into ten.

For this reason, with a madman attempting to steal Holly, Joshua was never more glad to have the funds at hand to hire an army of Bow Street runners or buy a hundred dogs, if that proved necessary to protect her.

"This is indeed serious," Finn muttered as Joshua ended his story.

"You can count on us, Josh. We'll help in any way we can," Tynan added. "I know Rawling is heir to a duke, but his title as marquess is still just a courtesy title. Whereas I am an earl in my own right. So are James and Marcus. If it helps to toss the weight of our ranks around, don't hesitate. And Caleb is still a general in the army. I know you're also in an important position, but you know he won't hesitate to back you up on any fighting forces you might need."

Ronan nodded. "Count me in, of course. If Romulus were here, he'd offer his frigate up as well. The Royal Navy is at your service."

Joshua grinned. "I'm not sure what the Lord Admiral will have to say about that."

Miranda, not to be outdone by her sons, huffed. "Leave that odious Lord Rawling to me. I've handled worse scoundrels in my day." She reached over and patted Holly's hand. "I'm glad Joshua brought you home to me. That wretch won't know what hit him if he dares approach you while you're here. I'll have his bollocks for breakfast if he tries it, sautéed in a wine sauce."

"Miranda!" Joshua groaned.

His brothers laughed. So did their wives.

Well, despite being beautiful and genteel, Belle and Abigail each had spirit. They'd been through their own hardships and would not shrink back or beg their husbands not to get involved. He liked that they were fighters.

Belle was Holly's cousin, and they'd always been close.

It did his heart good to see Holly smiling.

"I'll help you pour that wine into your frying pan, Miranda," Holly said.

Abigail smirked at her husband. "I think you ought to roast them."

Belle nodded. "Like chestnuts tossed on an open fire."

Finn groaned. "Enough, ladies. That is a tender subject for those of us who happen to be so equipped."

Joshua returned the discussion to their plans. "I hope you don't mind if we stay with you, at least for the next few days," he said to his mother. "I didn't want us returning to our new home as darkness fell. We have no live-in staff yet, and the house is empty. It would be easy enough for anyone to break in and hide in one of the rooms. I plan to go there tomorrow." He glanced at his brothers. "Ronan has to report to work, but I was hoping Finn or Tynan could come with me."

Miranda nodded. "And Holly will stay here with me."

"Yes, at least for now. I don't want her anywhere near the house until we have secured it."

"I'll come with you," Finn said.

"So will I." Tynan turned to his wife. "Abby, you don't need me for anything tomorrow, do you?"

"No. I'll come over here with you in the morning and pass the time with your mother and Holly until you return to fetch me."

"Oh, that's an excellent idea. I'll do the same," Belle said.

Ronan began to pace. "Blast, I want to go with you. They won't miss me if I report late, Josh."

Miranda frowned at Ronan. "No, you'll report to work."

He rolled his eyes. "Miranda, I am no longer an infant. You cannot tell me what to do."

She arched an eyebrow. "Are you married yet?"

"Oh, here it comes." Ronan already had that *help, get me out of here* look upon his face. "Don't start on me." He turned to Joshua. "This is your fault. She used to have the two of us to harass, but now you've abandoned me to face her on my own. And you, Finn. A few months ago, there were three of us against one of her. I'm not liking this situation at all."

Tynan laughed. "Holly, I understand you have *The Book of Love* now. Which explains why Joshua took about a minute to fall in love with you. Not that it was any different for Finn with Belle or Romulus with Violet. Slip it under Ronan's pillow while he's at work tomorrow. His bride will probably fall out of the sky and land on his head within an hour after you do." "Gad! You, too? Shut up, Ty." Ronan poured himself a brandy and ignored their mother's reprimand as he guzzled it down. "Leave me alone, Miranda. I'm not getting married anytime soon. I'll see you all tomorrow."

Miranda followed him out of the parlor. "Where are you going?"

"Out. Don't ask questions. You don't really want to know. It's nowhere suitable for ladies."

She returned to the parlor, looking not at all happy as her gaze took in all three of their wives. "Don't have sons. They are irascible, inconsiderate, and nothing but a bother."

Joshua winked at Holly. "You still like me, don't you, love?"

She blushed, and he realized he'd called her *love* in front of everyone. Not that he cared, for even he knew he was a doting fool around her. His brothers had all made love matches and knew exactly what was going through his mind—the worry for Holly's safety as well as the way his blood turned to fire whenever he was near her.

"Yes, Joshua. I find you quite tolerable."

He grinned. "Well, look at that. Four days married, and she still loves me."

But their light banter soon ended, and they spoke of their next steps in finding Lord Rawling. Serving Holly up as bait was ruled out for the moment, not that Joshua would ever permit it, even if everyone thought it was a good plan.

Things would have to be quite dire for him to change his mind on that.

"I'll meet with Homer Barrow tomorrow and fill him in on what happened in Harwich," he said. "Finn and I know from helping Belle and her sister when we were in Oxford that he and his Bow Street runners are men of many talents. I'll have him place two of his men in our house as footmen. It will ease my mind greatly to have them in the house once we settle in there, especially since I have to return to my post in a few days."

Tynan nodded. "As for dogs, I can bring one or two of ours down from the country. Sheba is my best scent dog, a beagle. She's too friendly to be a good guard dog, but her bark should be enough to alert everyone in the house if Rawling somehow makes his way in."

Joshua turned to Holly, curious as to how she was taking it all in. Her lips were pursed in thought, but she did not appear to be fretting so much as taking in the discussion. He placed his hand over hers, needing simply to hold on to her. His brothers certainly understood what he was feeling, and his mother, who was never known for holding back her feelings, would be the last one to complain. Quite the opposite, she was in raptures over her new daughters-in-law. "Miranda, the last item to discuss is what needs to be done for Holly to defend herself. Will you loan her one of your pistols and show her how to use it?"

His mother was surprisingly gentle when she turned to Holly. "My dear, I know you are not comfortable with this, but my son is right. We all will do everything in our power to protect you, but you also must be able to protect yourself."

Holly nodded. "I know. I was unwilling before, but I see there is no way around it."

When he and Holly retired to his old bedchamber later that evening, he studied her more closely as he helped her out of her gown. "What are you thinking, love?"

"I like the idea of protecting myself." She donned her nightrail and unbound her hair to brush it out before working it into a loose braid. "That ability is what will set me free, especially if Lord Rawling remains on the loose for months. I appreciate everything your family is doing for me, of course. But I will never have a normal life until I am confident enough to stop falling into panic at the sight of every moving shadow."

He disrobed as well and climbed into bed beside his wife, who had scrambled in as soon as she'd finished braiding her hair. "There are also ways to fight back when you are overpowered by someone larger than you. Our bodies have vulnerable spots. The throat, the eyes. For men, their…parts."

She grinned and raised the covers to glance at his. "You need never worry. I shall always treat yours delicately."

He shook his head and laughed. "As I shall always worship and adore yours. Come into my arms, love. We'll need a solid night's sleep. Tomorrow will be a busy day for us."

"Are we just going to sleep?"

"Mother in heaven, no. We can do whatever you wish to do. As you well know, when it comes to you, my low brain never turns off."

He silently resolved to claim her only the once because they would never sleep otherwise. But her body was the sweetest thing he'd ever tasted, and that resolution was quickly forgotten when she touched him a second time during the night. He buried himself in her sweet warmth and felt the fullness of her breasts against his chest, the softness of her lips on his, and lost himself in this beautiful girl he loved with all his being.

"I love you so much, Joshua."

"I love you double that." He kissed her brow as she lay snuggled in his arms. "Stop bewitching me and go to sleep, or we'll be dull as doorknockers come the morning."

But his own thoughts kept him awake much of the night.

Where was Rawling?

Was he back in London and now watching them?

CHAPTER SEVENTEEN

HOLLY WISHED SHE hadn't agreed to stay with Miranda while Joshua and his brothers went off to speak to Homer Barrow and then check on their new house. It was too late to change plans now that Abigail and Belle were here, too.

Abigail patted her hand as they sat in the parlor, and Miranda poured them each a cup of tea. "I know you want to be with Joshua, but it is easier for him to do whatever he needs to do without worrying about having you beside him."

"I know you're right. But it's very hard to sit here and do nothing all the while."

Miranda set down the teapot. "My dear, you needn't worry about that. I shall put you through your paces. First, learning how to handle a pistol. How to hold it, load it, clean it—for you never want to leave that responsibility to someone else—and lastly, how to shoot it properly. You want to hit the villain, not your neighbor's door or some poor coachman driving past in a carriage."

"Will you teach me, as well?" Belle asked, obviously as eager as Holly was for this training.

Abigail raised her hand politely. "Me, too. Please."

"Of course, my chicks." Miranda was in her element, leading her elegantly gowned troops. She would have made a fine general had women been permitted to serve in the army. All her sons thought so, too.

"Joshua spoke a little about tricks of defense. Do you know any of those?" Holly asked, feeling better now about having to sit home.

"Indeed, I do." Miranda was now beaming. "Pistol first. Then we shall all have lunch. Education in defense after lunch."

Joshua and his brothers returned in the early afternoon.

Holly and the other ladies were standing outdoors in the rear garden, in the square patch of grass between the flower beds that gracefully hugged the stone walls. Miranda was teaching them how to properly punch a man in the throat and then gouge his eyes. Her back was to her sons, so she did not see them watching her from the parlor window. "Follow with a swift knee between his legs. You want to drop him to the ground hard and fast. Your knee is your battle mace. Wield it without mercy."

Holly tried not to giggle as the men began to make faces, feigning mock agony as their mother went through the motions again, especially when she raised her knee. She, Belle, and Abigail lost their composure at the same time.

Miranda finally turned to see what had them holding their sides and tearing up with laughter. "Botheration, the wildebeests are back. Very well, ladies. Go fawn over those undeserving wretches, even if they are my sons, and I do love them."

They hurried to the parlor, all of them eager to hear what their husbands had to report. Holly was particularly excited to show Joshua all that Miranda had taught them. His expression softened as he took her into his arms and kissed her cheek. "Love," he said softly, "your eyes are sparkling."

She nodded. "Your mother is wonderful. She will have us battle-ready in no time. I wish Dahlia and Heather were here to learn this. I can't tell you how much calmer it has made me. Not that I will let down my guard for a moment, but I won't be terrified to go about my daily chores or walk outside…or face Lord Rawling if you are not there to protect me."

He kissed her again. "Much as I hate ever to leave your side, whenever I am not, rest assured someone else trustworthy will always be there. I've engaged two of Mr. Barrow's best men to serve as footmen. But don't ask too much of them. They're not hired to serve you so much as to guard you."

"Let's hear all of it, Joshua." Miranda motioned for the ladies to take their seats and gave a nod of approval when each son settled beside his wife. "How was the house? Any sign of entry?"

"No, it was untouched. We searched thoroughly inside and out. Rawling was too busy chasing after us to Harwich to break into the house. But it is something he might do tonight. I expect he'll be back in London by now, so the two Bow Street runners will be sleeping there and taking turns on night watch."

He took Holly's hand and gave it a light squeeze before returning his attention to Miranda. "We'll have to spend at least another two or three nights under your roof. I hope you don't mind."

His mother cast him a surprisingly affectionate smile. "You know it is my greatest pleasure. I'm delighted to have you and Holly with me."

"Thank you, Lady Miranda. My Aunt Sophie will help me hire a cook, maids, and a butler. More of our furniture should begin to arrive this week."

"So will your dog," Tynan said with grin. "I sent word off this morning to my estate manager."

"Meanwhile, Mr. Barrow has additional men posted to guard you personally, Holly. They're outside Miranda's house now. Teams of two at all times," Finn said. "Unfortunately, most of us don't know what Rawling looks like. We'd be more effective tracking him down if we had a better description of him. I understand the man has no prominent scars or other unusual features that would gain attention."

Belle and Holly exchanged glances. "Rose."

Joshua looked at her in confusion. "What?"

"Rose is our cousin," Holly said. "She is Aunt Sophie's daughter.

But she and Julian were not in London last week, and this is why she could not attend our wedding. Perhaps she is back now. She's an artist of extraordinary ability. I'll work with her to come up with a drawing of him. She can then sketch more drawings, as many as Mr. Barrow needs."

Miranda immediately rang for her butler. "Send word to Lady Chatham. We need to see her right away, and she must bring her sketchbook and drawing pencils."

Finn arched an eyebrow. "Miranda, we should have gone to her instead of summoning her to us."

His mother was unmoved. "Nonsense. There are seven of us here and only one of her there."

"She has children and a husband, not to mention her business and other responsibilities," Tynan said.

She called back her butler. "Griggs, hold off. I shall jot a letter to her. There, I hope you are all satisfied. I've invited her and Viscount Chatham to supper. You are all staying, of course. I don't wish to hear a word of protest." She returned her attention to her letter. "And bring a sketchbook and drawing pencils. There. Done. Hopefully they are home, and my efforts are not wasted."

Since Rose did not live far from Miranda's elegant residence, the messenger was back in short order. Griggs reported to Miranda immediately upon his return. "The viscount and viscountess are not in residence, nor are they expected to return to London for another fortnight."

"Damn," Joshua said, taking Holly's hand again.

She understood his frustration. They were all feeling the same. She and Joshua were the only ones who'd gotten a good look at the man. How could their Bow Street men hunt him down with a general description, at best?

Despite this disappointment, Holly was in better spirits as she and Joshua retired to his old bedroom. "Joshua, let me show you what

Miranda taught me. I'll merely go through the steps, not actually try to hurt you."

"Very well. Show me." He stepped closer, his nearness shooting tingles through her as always. She found it curious that this already handsome man grew even handsomer with each passing day. "I'll come up behind you and grab you."

She nodded and turned her back to him. "Just remember, Lord Rawling is not as big as you are."

"Right. I'll bend my knees to adjust my height. Ready, love?" When she nodded, he lightly clamped a hand on her mouth and trapped her arms with his free arm by wrapping it around her like a band of iron. He was gentle but firm. She could not turn to face him, or free her hand, or raise her arm to strike him in the throat. In pretense, of course. But he obviously wanted her to understand the difference in their strengths and learn how to overcome it.

She began to ask him questions as he eased his hand off her mouth. "You had me trapped. What could I have done?"

"Your first step should have been to figure out a way to get me to loosen my grip. You could have tried to sink your teeth into one of my fingers or any part of my hand. If Rawling ever has you, that's what you should do. Try to bite down as hard as you can."

She nodded. "And what if I can't?"

"He's standing behind you, that's how he would approach you in all likelihood because it will give him the element of surprise. If you can't bite him, then try suddenly going limp and falling forward. Deadweight, pardon the expression, is much harder to control than someone standing up and struggling. Give it a try, love."

He took her in his arms and nodded to her.

She allowed her body to go limp and immediately noticed the difference.

"While he expends his strength trying to regain his balance and lift you back against him, that's when you smack him in the face with your head. Hit his nose, if you can. But if he's too tall, then try to bash him under his chin."

"What else?"

"There are certain parts of the body that are tender and will respond reflexively. Sit down and let me show you."

When she took a chair, he told her to cross one leg over the other, and then he gently tapped her right below the kneecap. Her leg jumped. "Do you see? You had no control over that response. Love, get up, and let me come up behind you again. I'm not going to grab you, so just relax." He tapped behind her knees, and her legs suddenly gave way.

Joshua caught her, of course.

Holly was amazed and quite enjoying this lesson. "What did you just do?"

"I'm showing you more vulnerable spots on the body. If you hit them just right, your assailant will have no control over his response. Let's try this again. I will come up behind you and grab you as I did the first time. Try to bite my hand. If that fails, fall forward, then bring your head up sharply and smash my nose. Or under my chin. Remember, all you need to do is loosen my hold enough for you to turn around and punch me in the throat or poke my eyes. Once I'm blinded and struggling for breath, then you bring your knee up to my bollocks." He laughed as he went over the motions again. "Kindly do not use your full force on me. I'd like an heir or two before I'm turned into a eunuch."

"Oh, dear. We mustn't ever let that happen." She turned in his arms, her body suggestively rubbing along his as she faced him and gave him a searing kiss.

He groaned when the kiss ended, obviously aroused and eager to take it further. "Blessed saints. That would work, too."

"Ugh! I wouldn't consider it."

He raked a hand through his hair, his expression quite fierce and suddenly serious. "Love, I want you to do whatever you need to do to save yourself. If it means kissing him or rubbing yourself against his groin—"

"Joshua!"

"Save your life, Holly. I don't know if he means to harm you in that way, but you do whatever is necessary."

He was going to make her cry if he persisted. The thought of touching any other man in that way was unimaginable to her.

"The point is to use the element of surprise to get him to loosen his grip on you." He took her into his arms and held her tightly. "Do you think I will care what you do to escape that madman?"

"Please, Joshua. No more. Don't make me think of this possibility."

He sighed and kissed her gently on the brow. "Very well, love. We'll go back to lessons on beating him to a pulp."

She snuggled against him. "Yes, I like those much better. What else do you have to teach me?"

"Well, your legs are also weapons. If he knocks you to the ground, use your feet. Kick him in the bollocks or in the gut. Kick him in the knees. Don't stop kicking him, and if you can catch your breath while you are kicking the tar out of him, then scream at the top of your lungs and keep screaming until he runs off." He eased her out of his embrace and took hold of her shoulders so that she was directly facing him and meeting his gaze. "If he runs, you let him go. Do not chase after him. Will you promise me, Holly?"

She pursed her lips, not happy about this oath he was asking of her. "Would Wellington have allowed the enemy to retreat and not chased them at Waterloo? Would Julius Caesar have done the same at the battle of Alesia, allowing his Roman legions to sit idle while the Gauls got away?"

His eyes widened in surprise. "I am impressed by your knowledge of military history. But," he said with obvious exasperation, "you are small and slender. You are not Wellington or Caesar. The point is to escape him, not fall into his clutches again."

He caressed her cheek when she opened her mouth to offer more protest. "You know I would die inside if anything ever happened to you."

Reluctantly, she nodded. "I know. Very well, I promise."

How could she stay peeved when he was the most wonderful man in existence? "I think you've just gone through the lesson Miranda had planned for us tomorrow."

"Repetition can't hurt. And always keep your eyes out for a weapon to use."

"I will."

She tried out all he'd told her, softly so as not to hurt him.

"Well done, love." He came up behind her again.

"Is this still practice?"

He laughed. "No, this is just me desiring your body."

She turned in his arms, rubbing herself against him once more to purposely arouse him, although it really did not take much at all. "Good, and this is me seducing you. Is it working?"

"Hell, yes." He swept her up in his arms and carried her to bed.

"Joshua, we have our clothes on! They'll get wrinkled."

Before she knew it, his big hands were all over her, and in the next moment, she found herself undressed, and his lips were on her skin, fiery wherever he kissed her. "Blessed saints, I love your body," he said, his voice achy and rasping.

He removed his clothes, almost tearing them off in his eagerness to join her under the covers. When they coupled, she took the lead, enjoying being in control and watching Joshua's magnificent muscles flex and ripple, and his handsome face resplendent as he found his release.

He was awake and grinning at her when she opened her eyes the next morning. "Did you sleep well, love?" he asked, nuzzling her neck.

"Yes, very. Why are you smirking?" She caressed his cheek, running the palm of her hand along his rough stubble of beard.

"You were incredible last night. Utterly wild and wanton. My well-pleasured low brain is still in hot, twitching spasms."

Groaning, she slipped the covers over her head. "Is this any way to talk to your wife?"

He laughed and nudged the covers off her head. "Who else would I ever say it to? Only you, love. I marvel at my wisdom in falling in love with you. How do you feel this morning?"

"Wonderful. I won't ask you because your hyena grin says it all."

When she stretched, he emitted a moan and drew her up against his body. "I'd have at you again, but we have a lot to do today. Although I could be persuaded to stay abed a little while longer."

"No time for frolic." She sat up, modestly covering her body.

Joshua had no such qualms, obviously quite proud of his performance last night and feeling very conquering male about it. He tossed off his covers and rose to prepare himself for the day, not bothering to apply so much as a scrap of handkerchief to cover the most intimate parts of his body. "We'll spend most of the day at the house, interviewing applicants for our staff positions, and directing the movers as they deliver more furniture." He poured water from the ewer into the basin and picked up the soap beside it. "What time do you expect your Aunt Sophie?"

"Sometime in the late morning, about ten o'clock I'd say. Our first interview starts around that time, and Draper & Sons ought to be delivering our dining table and chairs. Dahlia and Heather will come by in the afternoon. Dahlia has more fabrics to show me for our curtains. She wants us to select colors and designs for our bedchamber, dining room, parlor, and the guest bedchambers."

He had been scrubbing his face with the soap, but quickly rinsed off and turned to her. "Shoot me now, and put me out of my misery. I'll leave that to you."

"Don't you care?"

"I care only that you like it." She tried not to gape as droplets of water slid down his neck. Really, she ought to be used to him by now, but he still stole her breath away. "Whatever pleases you, will please me."

"Must you always be so difficult?" she teased, scrambling out of bed and donning her robe. "Will you at least look at her suggestions for your office and the library? They're to be your domain mostly."

He nodded. "If it will make you happy."

"It will. Why are you in such a jolly humor today? You are so amenable to everything I say."

He picked up a towel and languidly wiped it across his chest. "Don't think too hard about it, love. My low brain is still in happy spasms. The Visigoths could be invading London, and I'd still be smiling and wanting to take you back to bed."

Joshua was dressed—finally—and seated at the breakfast table, having coffee with Lady Miranda by the time Holly had washed and dressed. She joined them in the breakfast room and placed a scone and jam on her plate.

Griggs came to her side as she took the seat beside Joshua, setting her plate down on the table. "Mint tea, Mrs. Brayden?"

She nodded. "Yes, thank you."

He poured her a cup and then returned to discreetly standing against the wall.

Ronan came down soon afterward, looking hungover, his condition given away by his watery, red eyes, obvious headache, and his mother's disapproving scowl. "Holly, you must find a lovely girl for Ronan to marry before he turns into a complete dissolute. Someone with an iron hand to keep him in line."

"I will not have a wife touching me with her cold, iron hand. Especially in winter. She'll freeze my—"

Miranda choked on her tea. "Ronan!"

"What? Holly's married now. And if I know Joshua, he's had her touching his—"

"I vow I shall kick you to Brighton and back if you say another word!" Miranda shot out of her chair. "Out! Off to work with you! You are Parliament's problem now. You'll fit right in with those witless baboons. Don't bother to come home until you are married. But to a nice girl like Holly, not one of your shameless tarts."

Ronan grabbed a sweet bun off one of the salvers. "Speaking of tarts." He bit into it. "Mmm, apple. Delicious. Holly, I'll make a deal with you. Find me a girl who tastes of cinnamon and apples, and I'll marry her."

Miranda rolled her eyes. "Women are not fruit to be plucked off a tree. You are hopeless. Be off with you."

Ronan came around the table and planted a kiss on his mother's cheek. "Love you to pieces, you henna-haired harpy."

Joshua coughed to cover his laughter.

Holly kicked him under the chair.

Sons were so different from daughters. However, she suspected not all mothers were quite like Miranda. She dished out twice as good as she got. It also had to be difficult for Ronan to suddenly find himself the sole bachelor among his brothers and cousins. Every wildebeest but him had now been tamed.

Which meant all eyes were on him.

Especially Miranda's keen, eagle eyes, and she was not going to take it easy on her son.

"Well, we had better be going, too. Are you ready, love?"

Holly nodded. "I'll just fetch my shawl. The sun's bright, but it feels a bit cool."

"Yes, do keep warm," Miranda said as Holly turned to leave. "I'll be along later as well, but only for a short while. Abigail and Belle are coming over about four o'clock for more lessons. Then we'll have tea. If Joshua is not ready to leave your new house at that time, then you can hop in the carriage with me. I don't want you to miss my next instruction."

Joshua tipped his head in assent. "I doubt we will stay beyond that hour. The sun will be setting by then, and I don't want Holly in the house after dark. Not that I'm overly worried about her now. You've turned her into a Valkyrie."

Holly rolled her eyes. "Nonsense. One day's training is not enough to turn me into a warrior. I'll be right back."

She ran upstairs to fetch her shawl. She'd given the others she'd acquired at Mrs. Mullins's shop in Harwich as gifts to the ladies in the family. But she'd kept the aquamarine one for herself because it perfectly matched the color of her eyes.

She walked to her room with a light step and had no sooner opened the door and taken a step in than someone grabbed her from behind.

Lord Rawling! How did he get in here?

CHAPTER EIGHTEEN

HOLLY FELT LORD Rawling's clammy hand clamp over her mouth before she could scream. One of his wiry arms came around her body to pin her arms down. She could not help but inhale the foul scent of his breath as he spoke against her ear. "We meet again, Mrs. Gleason."

She tried to shout at him to let her go, but her words were muffled and unintelligible.

He laughed cruelly. "You cannot escape me."

His entire body was foul and rank, the odor unbearable. He hadn't washed in days, too busy chasing them from London to Harwich and back. Her mind reverted to utter panic when he began to drag her to the panel leading to the servants' stairs. It was open just a crack, obviously the way he'd gotten into her bedchamber and meant to sneak her out.

She wanted to believe it was a trick.

"Let me go!" she shouted again, but her voice was swallowed in the palm of his hand. This man was sick and putrid in body and mind. She revolted at the thought of his being able to break into Lady Miranda's house in spite of all the protections surrounding her.

How was it possible?

She wanted to believe it was a prank, that Joshua was testing her again.

But she knew he would never do such a thing, never allow anyone to hold her so roughly or scare her this way. *Joshua! Joshua! Where are you?*

She'd just left him downstairs. How long would it take him to notice she was gone too long?

Her entire body began to shake.

Her heart pounded so hard, she could hardly breathe.

Think.

Clear your head.

"There's no point in struggling, Mrs. Gleason." His voice sounded high pitched and eerily thin as he dragged her toward that open panel. Despite her struggles, he'd already dragged her halfway across the room.

She tried to scream again, but her voice was still muffled by his hand across her mouth. He continued to ramble. "I need Walter's forgiveness. He's dead, and it is all my fault. You and I are going to him."

She shook her head wildly.

What did he mean by that? Did he intend to take her to Walter's grave? It was in York. Days away. Or was he going to kill her and carry her body north to dump atop Walter's gravestone?

"You must tell him. He's angry and won't speak to me."

Mother in heaven! Had he been trying to talk to a corpse?

"Mrs. Gleason, he must be made to understand. I never meant to hurt him or my brother."

She hated being called that.

She was Mrs. Brayden now.

"Why won't he talk to me? Why won't he forgive me?"

She wanted to tell him that he was not at fault. No one had ever blamed him for Walter's death or that of his brother. But his mind was now so twisted, even if she went down on her knees and swore she and Walter had forgiven him, he would never believe her.

Think.

She'd stood in this very spot last night with Joshua's arms around her. *Bite his hand.* She worked her mouth, but could not sink her teeth into any part of his skin. What was next? Don't struggle. *Go limp and fall forward.* She did just that and was surprised when Lord Rawling's grip loosened as he was caught off guard and almost dropped her.

He was now off balance and trying to secure his hold on her. She purposely stuck her leg out so that his legs got tangled in hers, and he tripped. He released her as he fell, the instinct to hold out his arms to break his fall, overcoming the need to abduct her in that instant.

It was all the time she needed.

She rolled away and began screaming at the top of her lungs.

The bedroom door was closed, and Joshua was downstairs. Would he hear her? Would anyone hear her? She tried to run to the door, but Lord Rawling, even though he was now on the ground, had managed to grab her ankle and had a painful hold of it.

He was strong in his determination, pulling her back as she struggled to break free and run away.

She continued to scream. "Joshua! Joshua!"

Were he not so deranged, he would have let her go to escape before he was caught. But his mind was not clear, and he was obsessed with abducting her.

Mother in heaven.

Perhaps he was obsessed with killing her.

Lord Rawling's grip was too tight.

He still would not let her go.

She saw the glint of a blade in his hand.

Now she understood, he meant this to be the end for both of them. In his deranged mind, he wished to close the circle. Stanford and Walter had died together. Now she and Rawling would do the same.

She turned and kicked him as hard as she could in the face. Then she stomped on his belly and kicked him in the face again, this time going for his nose. As he raised the knife to stab her leg, she stomped down on his male parts as hard as she could.

The knife fell from his hand as he released it to clutch his privates. Holly kicked the blade under her bed and grabbed the candlestick off her nightstand. She had just turned and raised it to hit him with it when the door flew open with a crash, and Joshua burst into the room. Following on his heels were Griggs and two burly footmen. They stared at Lord Rawling writhing on the floor. They looked back at her with her heaving chest, and the candlestick raised over her head.

Joshua's mouth gaped open. "Holly, you did this?"

He was staring at Lord Rawling, still writhing.

She nodded, unable to speak as she was still struggling to catch her breath.

His gaze was so full of love and aching relief. "Stay back, my beautiful Valkyrie."

He grabbed the fiend by the scruff of his neck and hauled him to his feet. Lord Rawling was now the one in panic. He lashed out wildly, but Joshua ducked his every punch so that he was merely swinging at air.

Joshua's fists were the size of cannonballs and packed as much force. He finally threw a punch of his own that caught Lord Rawling solidly in the jaw and would have knocked him out had Joshua not held back.

She wasn't sure why he hadn't unleashed all his fury. Perhaps because they were looking at a shell of a man, now nothing more than a frail, wounded creature. "It is over, my lord," Joshua said. "Fight me, and I will kill you with my bare hands. You know I am capable of doing it."

Joshua twisted Lord Rawling's arms behind his back and began giving orders to Griggs and his two footmen. These footmen were obviously hired for their size and brawn. Although as far as Holly was concerned, no one was as splendid as Joshua.

After searching Lord Rawling for weapons and finding none, Joshua turned to the others. "Get him out of here, and tie him to a chair in the dining room. Damn, I wish we had a dungeon in this house. I'd toss him into the darkest pit."

He frowned as he surveyed the room and saw the open panel used by servants to enter the room unobtrusively. "Griggs, wait! How did this bastard get to the servants' stairs?"

Their trusted butler turned ashen. "I have no idea, Captain Brayden. I'll question the staff immediately."

"Give me a moment, and I'll do it with you." He made a quick search of the room and servants' stairs to make sure no one else was lying in wait. "For now, secure Lord Rawling. Have your men stand guard over him. They are not to take their eyes off him for a moment, not even once he's bound. He is deranged and dangerous. Do not underestimate his cunning."

"Understood, Captain Brayden."

"Send a messenger to the Duke of Ismere's residence. Let him know we have his son, and he must come at once." He raked a hand through his hair in consternation. "In the meanwhile, I'll find out what happened to the two Bow Street runners who should have been outside the house standing guard over my wife."

Joshua stood beside her while Griggs and the footmen led a dazed, but still struggling Lord Rawling downstairs.

As soon as they were gone, he emitted a groan that seemed to tear from the depths of his soul and hauled her into his arms. He hugged her fiercely, not caring that with her candlestick still raised, she almost hit him in the head. "Love, are you all right?"

She nodded, finally dropping her arm and setting aside the candlestick. "Yes, I did everything you taught me last night, and it worked."

"You were incredibly brave. Thank the Lord, you're all right. Are you sure he didn't hurt you?"

"He scared me, that was all. I kicked his knife under the bed. Let me—"

Joshua's eyes rounded in alarm. "He had a knife? Blessed saints!

How did you disarm him?"

"It fell out of his hands when I stomped on...I stomped hard between his legs, as you taught me."

He hugged her fiercely again and kissed her on the lips, on her cheeks, her eyes, her brow. "I love you, Holly."

"Feeling is mutual, my handsome captain."

He kissed her again.

His hands were shaking as he released her. "He might have killed you."

She cupped his face and tipped his head down for another kiss. "Not a chance, my love. I have no intention of turning you into an eligible widower so soon. But I think it would have been quite different if you hadn't given me the confidence to do what I needed to do to save myself. I hope Miranda will be proud of me, too."

"She will be." He nodded. "I want to stay here and hold you into eternity, but there's more to do. Those Bow Street runners might be missing. Possibly hurt. And there's an investigation to conduct into who let Rawling in."

Holly went over to their bed and bent down to grab the knife that she'd kicked under it only a few moments ago. It felt as though hours had passed. Perhaps it had been two minutes. "We'd better check on your mother as well. The incident must have overset her."

"We do need to check on her, but only to make certain she hasn't beaten Rawling to death before his father arrives."

He would not allow Holly to come outside with him while he searched for the missing Bow Street men. He left her in his mother's care and was relieved when Holly did not protest. He had just gone out of the servants' entrance and started to search amid the shrubs on the side of the house when he saw the two runners lying motionless behind a row boxwood. "Bollocks," he muttered, knowing Rawling could not have done this on his own.

At first, he feared they had been killed. But upon checking for a pulse on each, he realized they were merely unconscious. Each had a strong pulse. No sign of blood. Likely they had been hit over the head and dumped out of sight.

He removed the pistol always kept in the lip of his boot and cautiously made his way into the rear alley. Two big men were standing in wait beside a wagon. He was a big man himself, but these oxen were imposing in size, even for him. They looked nasty, too. Weathered, leathery faces crisscrossed with scars. Big, beefy fists.

One of them carried a whip.

Joshua raised his weapon and trained it on the man's chest. "Unless you wish to be hanged along with the gentleman who hired you, I suggest you leave London immediately and never come back."

The blackguard with the whip appeared to consider the warning. But he was about to come to the wrong conclusion. His friend tried to set him right. "His lordship ain't paid us yet, Len. I'm not stayin' around to hang for the likes o' him. He ain't right in the head. Let's get out o' here before the patrol arrives."

His friend raised his arm to snap his whip, so Joshua cocked his pistol. "Don't be daft, Len. Do as your friend says."

"That's right, Len. Do it," the first man said in a pleading voice. "All we done was cosh them two runners over the head. No one's gonna come after us for that. Put down yer whip or he'll shoot ye."

"Too late, gentlemen."

Joshua felt some disappointment in not having taken them down on his own. He would have liked to throw a few punches, but the neighborhood patrol was now here. He'd let them deal with the two ruffians. As the first man said, they hadn't been paid and were not about to do Rawling's bidding.

They'd have to answer for the two injured runners, but they hadn't killed these men. Joshua wasn't sure why they hadn't. No doubt the reason was the same, they hadn't been paid. "Thank goodness for that," he muttered to himself.

Griggs and another able footman came running toward him. "The Duke of Ismere is on his way," Griggs said, out of breath.

The footman was carrying a shotgun and joined the patrol in holding down Len and his confederate. By the shouts and sounds of scuffling as they were marched around the corner and out of his sight, Joshua knew the blackguards were now desperately trying to escape custody. "Griggs, send a messenger to Homer Barrow, and ask him to come here as soon as possible. And we'd better summon Dr. Farthingale to have a look at Mr. Barrow's men."

"I'll take care of it at once, Captain Brayden."

When Joshua returned to the house, he was shocked to find Holly talking to Rawling. Of course, the two footmen and Miranda were there as well, and Rawling was tied to the chair.

Still, Joshua did not like that she was even in the same room with him. As he approached to take her out of there, Miranda silently motioned for him to stay still. "You must let her confront him," she whispered, "or your soft-hearted wife will always fret about what she ought to have done."

He nodded. Yes, this was Holly's way, to hold things in and let them eat at her insides. He was surprised his mother understood her nature so well.

"You must allow your pain to heal, Lord Rawling," Holly said, her voice so gentle it made Joshua ache for the fright this villain had given her. "You are not to blame for the deaths of your brother or my late husband."

Rawling began to whimper.

It was a frightening sound to Joshua's ears, but Holly did not appear to be affected by it and continued to talk to him in her gentle manner. "If it is forgiveness from me that you seek, then I do forgive you. But their deaths were not your fault. Never your fault. I also forgive you on behalf of Walter. He is at peace. He is in heaven with your brother. Their spirits are bound forever. It is as it should be. I do not think they could have lived one without the other."

Joshua studied Rawling's eyes, saw the anguish in them.

She'd spoken to him calmly and compassionately, but Rawling was deranged. He was nodding and thanking Holly, if his frail whines could be called that. But Joshua could see the calculation in his eyes.

As soon as Holly had finished, he drew her away.

Hell and damnation, he wanted this to be over.

He wanted them to set up a household, raise a family. He wanted her to enjoy the simple entertainments, to take her to those interminable musicales that were so popular during the Season, and glittering balls and merry dinner parties. He wanted to grow old with her.

Lord Rawling's father arrived shortly afterward with his own Bow Street men and two others who were introduced as doctors, although Joshua was in doubt about them. They had none of the refinement of George Farthingale. In truth, they sent chills up Joshua's spine, and he wasn't the one they were taking away.

He could not help but feel sorry for Rawling. Yet, never that sorry. He'd stalked Holly and tried to hurt her.

He'd meant to do worse if that knife she'd kicked out of his hands was any indication.

The two so-called doctors bound Rawling in a jacket that pinned his arms to his body and then escorted him out. Rawling appeared spent, resigned to being restrained. But that cold calculation in his eyes still had Joshua on edge.

He turned to the duke once his son was out of his hearing. "Your Grace, what's to become of him now?"

"He'll be confined to my estate at Ismere and made as comfortable as possible for his last days. You must have noticed his gaunt appearance. He is sick physically as well as…"

Joshua nodded. "His eyes appear hollow, and his complexion is alarmingly yellow."

"There is no meat left on his bones. The sickness has eaten him up inside, so there is nothing left of him but diseased skin over fragile bones."

"Perhaps it is this physical sickness that has also attacked his mind," Holly said with concern.

"I believe it is, but who can know such things? Mrs. Brayden, what was he blabbering about as his doctors led him out? He said something about forgiveness."

"Yes, he needed to know I forgave him for Walter's death. I never blamed him for it, and I don't know if he will ever believe me. I hope he does. His mind is so tortured."

The duke took her hand and kissed it. "I hope he does, as well. I cannot bear to see him as he is now. But he'll be at peace soon enough. He won't live to see the winter. He might not survive the journey to Ismere, he is that near the end." He cast her a mirthless smile. "I think this ought to bring you relief, Mrs. Brayden, after all my son has put you through."

"Yes, relief," Holly admitted. "But no joy in his suffering."

"Indeed, there is no joy in this whole affair. But rest assured, he will be confined and never be a threat to you again." The duke then turned to Joshua. "Come see me tomorrow."

"I will, Your Grace."

Joshua put his arms around Holly as they stood on the front steps and watched the duke's carriage disappear down the street. "You're shivering, love. Let me take you inside."

"No, I'll be all right with your arms around me to keep me warm. I don't want to go in just yet. I need to feel the bite of air against my cheeks."

They were still on the front steps when Homer Barrow and Holly's uncle arrived within moments of each other. Holly's uncle arrived first, and she flung herself into his arms. "Uncle George, I'm so glad you're here."

His brow furrowed in concern. "What has happened? Are you

hurt?"

"No, not me. Mr. Barrow's men were knocked out. Ah, here's Mr. Barrow now."

Joshua and Holly took them both inside so they could tend to the Bow Street runners, who were now conscious, although unsteady on their feet. "The neighborhood patrol has Lord Rawling's accomplices in custody now," Joshua said as the runners were being examined. "I'll leave the matter of their punishment to you, Mr. Barrow. How badly are they hurt, Dr. Farthingale?"

"They'll recover. Nasty lumps, but I've seen much worse. They must rest for a week, I would say. No strenuous activities."

Homer nodded. "We'll do exactly as you say. I'm grateful, Dr. Farthingale."

Joshua checked his watch. It was almost ten o'clock. He and Holly had arranged to interview household staff. But he still hadn't interviewed Miranda's staff to find out who'd let Rawling in.

Holly must have realized the time, for she suddenly gasped. "The interviews! Oh, Joshua, it is the last thing I want to do today."

Miranda took her gently by the shoulders and steered her into the parlor. "Of course, my dear. You won't do any such thing. You'll stay right here and rest. I'll go in your place. Your Aunt Sophie and I shall take care of everything. Never you worry."

Joshua arched an eyebrow, dubious about the two matriarchs taking over their tasks, but Holly seemed to have no problem with it. "I would rely on their experience anyway before making any choices," she said. "I don't mind handing over the task to them, at least for today."

Miranda turned to Joshua. "I have my suspicions as to who let Rawling in here. If this girl is missing when you question the kitchen staff, then you'll have your culprit. She's one of the new scullery maids taken in from St. Mary's Orphanage. You know we've done this for years, provided employment for these girls and boys to give them a start in life. Polly is her name. I felt it my charitable duty to engage her services, give her a chance to make something of herself, but she has proven herself to be lazy. Mrs. Harold recently complained of items being pilfered from her kitchen."

Miranda regarded both of them, her expression quite pained. "Stealing a few sausages or a mixing spoon is one thing. I never thought she would be so coldhearted as to allow a murderer into my home. This is all my fault."

Joshua frowned. "No, it isn't. Rawling was going to find a way in, no matter how careful we were. If it wasn't Polly, then he would have found someone else. You couldn't have sacked her on the chance she would do such a thing. We'll see what turns up. It might not have been her at all."

But as it turned out, it was. Polly had run off this morning, but not before bragging to the other scullery maids of coming into a bit of money.

"Well, that ties up all the loose ends," he said, escorting Holly into the parlor to give them a moment to themselves.

Holly, being methodical and organized by nature, began to count off everything they'd accomplished. "Miranda is at our new house to meet the hopefuls applying for positions. Sophie will have joined her there by now. Uncle George has treated the runners. You've hired a hack to drive them back to Mr. Barrow's office. The duke and those awful men have taken Lord Rawling away. His accomplices are now under arrest. Will you bother to search for Polly?"

"Yes, Mr. Barrow will try to locate her whereabouts. But I doubt she'll stay in London once she realizes Rawling's intent was abduction and murder, not theft. She knows she'll be hanged if she's ever brought back here. If he doesn't find her by the end of the week, we'll not pursue it. Unless she changes her ways, I have no doubt she'll be dead or imprisoned for some other misdeed soon."

She began to nibble her lip and fret again.

"What is it, love?"

"Lord Rawling is ill and dying. I thought I'd defended myself well and felt quite powerful for it. But I wasn't really. All I did was fight off a weak, sick man." She sank onto the settee, her spirits suddenly deflated.

He sat beside her and took her hand. "That man was smart enough to outwit all of us and strong enough to hurt any of us."

"Not you."

"Even me." He cast her a wry grin. "But you'd kicked the tar out of him before I ever got close, so there was nothing for me to do but restrain him. His evil gave him strength. You defended yourself magnificently. But I knew you would." He grinned again. "I've felt your wallop. You're dangerous with a candlestick."

"Don't remind me." She finally managed a laugh. "I never got the chance to hit him with it. You burst in before I could."

His manner turned serious for a moment. "Don't ever doubt yourself, Holly. You rose to the challenge as few others could. Afterward, you showed kindness and compassion few others would. This is why I love you and will always love you."

He paused a moment, and his grin returned. "Not to mention, you have a face and body that drops me to my knees every time I look at you. But that is an altogether separate matter. It only proves how wise I am in recognizing your perfection."

She laughed. "And now that we've decided you are incredibly brilliant, what shall we do for the rest of the day? And I don't mean spending it in bed. I'd like to join Sophie and Miranda at our new house. I think I need to turn my mind toward our future and not dwell on all that has happened today or in the past. Would you mind?"

"Not at all. Let's walk over. It isn't too far, and a stroll through the park will do us both good."

"And perhaps stop at a tea shop along the way?"

"Yes, whatever you wish."

"You're being very agreeable."

"Relieved is more like it. Thanking the Graces you are safe and unharmed. This is your day. We shall do whatever it is you'd like to do."

"Even visit my Aunt Hortensia?"

Joshua lifted her onto his lap and kissed her soundly on the lips. "Gad, who knew you were so cruel? Yes, even visit Hortensia, if that is truly your wish."

She put her arms around his neck. "No, we shall see her soon enough. Aunt Sophie and Uncle John are hosting a party this coming Saturday. We're invited, of course. So are your brothers and Miranda. I look forward to the day we can host them all in our own home."

"It will be soon."

She scooted off his lap. "Let's go, my handsome captain. I think I need to keep very busy today or I may burst into tears as everything hits me all at once. I just have to get my shawl...I...I..."

"Oh, hell." This is what she'd run up to fetch when Rawling had attacked her. Joshua took her back in his arms. "Holly, love. Let it out. I'm right here."

"No, I want to be strong and brave." But she was trembling now and held out her hands in dismay. "I don't want to cry, even if it is out of relief."

"One thing has nothing to do with the other. Tears running down your cheeks will not change the fact that you bested a villain. But if it makes you feel better, you may kiss me every time you feel the urge to cry. I shall endure as many kisses as you wish to toss at me."

"How very considerate of you." But she laughed. Then she reached up and kissed him on the lips. "Thank you. It is an excellent idea." She kissed him again.

He lifted her up against him and kissed her so deeply, she felt his kiss to the depths of her soul. "I'll retrieve the shawl for you," he said upon ending the kiss. "Or I can accompany you upstairs and stand beside you while you fetch it."

She nodded. "I like the idea of you standing beside me."

"Always, love. You know that." He offered his arm to her. "Care to give it a try? Or do you need another moment?"

She placed her arm in his. "No more moments."

He allowed her to take the lead and adjusted his pace to hers as they climbed the stairs. Waited for her to open their bedroom door. But once the door was open, he asked, "Love, do you want me to go in first?"

She took a deep breath. "No, I must do it."

A maid was tidying up the room when they walked in. She bobbed a curtsy and turned to leave through the servants' stairs, but Holly called her back. "It's all right. Stay, please. I'm just collecting my shawl."

She grabbed it and wrapped it over her shoulders, then cast Joshua a triumphant smile.

He smiled back, his gaze a mix of tenderness and pride.

"I know it is a small thing, but I'm glad I managed it."

He took her hand in his as they walked back downstairs. "No, it is a huge thing. No different from the fears any soldier might have when hearing a sudden noise. A pistol fired. Even watching a fireworks display. Everyone might be looking up in wonder and cheering each fiery burst. But there are those in the audience with false smiles frozen on their faces, who are sweating and wishing it would all end soon because it reminds them of the battles in which they fought and their terror as the enemy fell upon them."

Griggs was standing at the entry with Holly's cloak in hand. Joshua took it and wrapped it around her. He waited until they'd walked out of the house to continue the conversation. "I think this is why I knew I loved you the moment I touched you. It wasn't merely a low-brain response, although there is always that with you. But I've figured out the rest of it."

She smiled at him. "Just what have you figured out?"

"A calming warmth filled me when I set my hands on you. It was as though my body was telling me in that instant, *You've found her. She is the one who will take away your pain and fears.*"

He shook his head. "It was most odd, really. There you were wielding that candlestick and bringing it down upon my head."

"Ugh! I forbid you from ever mentioning it again. I'd rather talk about something else. Anything else."

"Such as what?"

The day was cool but filled with sunshine, and their walk along the park was quite pleasant. Holly felt as though she was back in the countryside, for the lovely green grass and trees that were changing color. The vivid reds and golds against the blue sky were quite magnificent. The hardier mums were still blooming in their flower beds.

He looked quite splendid as he walked beside her. "Joshua."

"What, love?" His head dipped toward her.

She took the opportunity to give him a quick kiss on the cheek even though they were out in public. "It's time for me to hand off *The Book of Love.*"

"Ah, that magical tome you believe brought us together."

"It did, even though you were the one to read it and tell me what it said. But I'm not certain who to pass it on to next."

"Ronan will be disappointed. He wanted to read it."

"I think it must go to Dahlia. She's the logical choice to have it next, but she has a beau in York. He is in London now, and I expect he will soon propose to her now that she has come of age. Perhaps she will hand it off to Ronan after she reads it."

"I'll tell him to ask her." They crossed a busy thoroughfare, safely reaching the other side before he responded. "But back to Dahlia's beau, you are assuming he is the right match for her."

She nodded. "He's been courting her forever."

Joshua shrugged. "And been a complete gentleman about it?"

"Yes, I believe so. Dahlia and Heather tell me everything." She grimaced. "It feels churlish now, knowing that I hid so much from them."

"You had your reasons. I'm sure you gave them good advice whenever they took you into their confidence."

"I tried my best. Why did you ask if he's been a complete gentleman?"

"Because no man who is truly in love can ever be a gentleman around the woman he loves. Low brain, love. It takes over. *Mine. No one else can have her.* We turn into baboons, baring our teeth and showing off our big, red arses to scare off our competitors."

She laughed. "You've read my cousin Lily's monographs on baboon behavior. She'll be so pleased."

"Your cousin is brilliant. Were she a man, she'd probably be a Fellow in the Royal Society or a chancellor in charge of one important government ministry or another. But to get back to the subject of that book and who should get it next, I think you must give it to Dahlia. If her Yorkshire beau is meant for her, then they will find a way to be together."

"But if he isn't…"

Joshua grinned. "Then I look forward to the mayhem certain to ensue as your sister finds her true love. She is a Farthingale, after all. Never a dull moment with you. I doubt a single one of you has had a traditional courtship."

"I'm sure one of us…well, perhaps not." Holly cast him an impish grin. "Would you think less of me if I agreed with you? I need a good laugh right now. And come to think of it, for Dahlia to accept Gerald Wainscott and set a date for her traditional wedding, a date which likely won't be until sometime next year, is quite troubling. I knew I'd be wanton with you the moment I caught sight of you in all your manly glory. I would have become a terrible sinner if we hadn't married right away. So I must thank you for making an honest woman of me."

He laughed. "My pleasure. And believe me, you've given me pleasure beyond my wildest fantasies. I've come out the winner in this."

"Oh, Joshua. This is what I want for Dahlia. She deserves a husband whose eyes light up whenever she enters a room. Yes, you've convinced me. She must get *The Book of Love* next."

They passed several tea shops on the way to their new Mayfair home, but Holly was now looking forward to setting up their household and eager to see who Miranda and Sophie had interviewed. She was also eager to see what furniture had been delivered and looked forward to selecting more fabrics with Dahlia, who really did have a wonderful eye for design.

As they arrived at their front gate, the sun was still shining. Joshua paused to give her a kiss. "I love you, Holly. Welcome home."

"I love you more, my handsome captain." She gave Joshua a short but ardent kiss on the lips, one that would be considered quite scandalous if they were seen by their new neighbors. "But I have one more question for you."

"Yes, love?"

"If Gerald Wainscott isn't Dahlia's true love, then who do you think it might be?"

CHAPTER NINETEEN

London, England
December 1820

HOLLY GAVE JOSHUA a slight nudge in his ribs as they stood together, watching over their guests while hosting their first party. "That's Gerald Wainscott," she whispered, "he's walking in beside Dahlia now. The young man with the curled blond hair."

It was an afternoon tea. The friends and family remaining in town over the yuletide season had been invited to attend. Holly was particularly eager to show off their home and all they had done to decorate it.

Rose and her husband had given them a beautiful tea service as a wedding gift, which was now on proud display in the dining room, the teapots with matching cups, saucers, and creamers set up on a table that spanned one wall. For the men or those who preferred a heartier drink than tea, a bowl of mulled wine and decanters of port had also been set up beside the tea service.

"What do you think of him, Joshua?" she asked, tucking her arm in his as they strolled from room to room to chat with their guests.

Another table laden with cold ham glazed with honey, a stubble goose stewed in plum juices, salted fish, venison, game birds, boiled turnips, and a mash of potatoes and onions had been set up on the opposite wall. A third table along the back wall held lighter fare, plum pudding, mincemeat pies, spiced apple tarts, scones with sultanas, and clotted cream.

Joshua rolled his eyes. "Oh, lord. Don't drag me into your match-making schemes."

Aunt Sophie's cook, the inimitable Mrs. Mayhew, had prepared a Twelfth Night cake, although it was not even Christmas yet, but fun anyway. She'd put a dried bean and a dried pea in it so that the man who got the bean in his slice would be king of the tea party, and the woman who got the pea would be queen. As king and queen, they would be the ones to open the dancing and would have to share that first dance together.

Usually, she and Joshua would have taken on that role, but they thought it would be fun to have Queen Pea and King Bean take it over instead. Everyone was in good spirits and not minding this traditional bit of silliness, even if it was still too early in the month for it.

Holly sighed. "I'm not matchmaking. I'm merely asking for your opinion." She batted her eyelashes at him and cast him a flirtatious smile. "Because you are my wise husband, and I adore you. Your opinion matters to me."

"Lord, you have me wrapped around your little finger. Our guests are just arriving, and I already wish they'd go so I can have you all to myself. You look beautiful, Holly."

She had on an ivory tea gown with an overlayer of pale pink sarcenet. "Thank you, my handsome captain. But I would still like an answer. What do you think of Gerald Wainscott? Be honest. This is important to me. I gave Dahlia *The Book of Love* yesterday. She wasn't keen to have it, said she didn't need it, and Ronan could have it if he still wanted it. I gave it to her anyway. It's up to her what she does with it now. Now tell me, do we like Gerald or not?"

"He looks a bit affected, don't you think? Who stands in front of a mirror and tediously fashions every curl into place other than fops and dandies?"

She poked him again. "It is all the style. All the young men are wearing their hair this way."

"No Brayden male ever would. It is affected. I don't like him already."

"Joshua!"

"Well, you said you wanted the truth."

She sighed again. "Yes, but I'm almost sorry I asked. No one can ever live up to a Brayden. Doesn't Dahlia look pretty? Heather, too."

He cast her an indulgent smile. "Yes, love. Come with me a moment. There's something we forgot to do."

"We did? I was sure we'd thought of everything." But she did not resist when he took her hand and led her down the hall to his library.

He pulled her in and took her into his arms. "We forgot this." He kissed her with all his heart and soul. "Have I mentioned how much I love you?"

"Not in the last five minutes. I was bereft, thinking you no longer cared for me." She giggled and then kissed him back with equal fervor, loving the warmth of his mouth on hers and the confidence in his probing lips and wickedly roaming hands.

They stayed in the library longer than intended, and Holly needed assistance in putting herself back together when they finally drew away from each other. Joshua's clothing needed a little straightening out as well.

Perhaps they'd been too taken up in the moment.

But they were hurriedly brought back to attention when they heard a chorus of cheers and hearty applause coming from the dining room. "Joshua, what do you think that is?"

"I have no idea. But it sounded quite merry. Nothing to be alarmed about. Let's find out."

Their guests had formed a circle around a couple that Holly could not yet make out because she was not tall enough to see over most heads. She had to squeeze her way between bodies to reach the couple.

It turned out King Bean and Queen Pea had been found. Joshua's brother, Ronan, had found the bean in his slice of cake. Dahlia had gotten the pea in her slice.

"Oh, my goodness." Holly looked up at Joshua, unable to contain her mirth. "Should we tell them? Do they realize?"

He grinned back at her. "No, my love. Don't say a word. Just stand back and watch the mayhem begin."

Also by Meara Platt

FARTHINGALE SERIES
My Fair Lily
The Duke I'm Going To Marry
Rules For Reforming A Rake
A Midsummer's Kiss
The Viscount's Rose
Earl Of Hearts
If You Wished For Me
Never Dare A Duke
Capturing The Heart Of A
Cameron

BOOK OF LOVE SERIES
The Look of Love
The Touch of Love
The Taste of Love
The Song of Love
The Scent of Love
The Kiss of Love
The Chance of Love
The Gift of Love
The Heart of Love
The Hope of Love (novella)

DARK GARDENS SERIES
Garden of Shadows
Garden of Light
Garden of Dragons
Garden of Destiny

THE BRAYDENS
A Match Made In Duty
Earl of Westcliff
Fortune's Dragon
Earl of Kinross
Pearls of Fire*
(*also in Pirates of Britannia series)
Aislin
Gennalyn

DeWOLFE PACK ANGELS
SERIES
Nobody's Angel
Kiss An Angel
Bhrodi's Angel

About the Author

Meara Platt is a USA Today bestselling author and an award winning, Amazon UK All-star. Her favorite place in all the world is England's Lake District, which may not come as a surprise since many of her stories are set in that idyllic landscape, including her award-winning paranormal romance Dark Gardens series. If you'd like to learn more about the ancient Fae prophecy that is about to unfold in the Dark Gardens series, as well as Meara's lighthearted, international bestselling Regency romances in the Farthingale series, Book of Love series, and the Braydens series, please visit Meara's website at www.mearaplatt.com.

Made in the USA
Columbia, SC
16 June 2025

59495802R10115